THE
FREEDOM
BUILDING

Martin Kendall

For more information, address:
mkendall80@yahoo.co.uk

Book cover design by BEAUTeBOOK
Paperback first edition 2020
ISBN: 978-1-9162990-1-6
www.martinkendall.com

THE
FREEDOM
BUILDING

1

John Gowan didn't like summing up his life but did it constantly: He was forty-eight years old. He was an architect. He built his house in the leafy countryside between the towns of Blanworth and Toxon. He grew up in Blanworth, had a contented childhood with decent parents – now deceased – and happy memories from school. He met his future wife at college and, a few years later, they had a daughter. But the marriage disintegrated and, when his daughter grew up, his wife left him. He hadn't spoken to either of them for a long while. His wife spent his money on holidays to New Zealand and lived with friends. He would be getting a divorce soon.

'Go on, overtake me!' he said, looking into his rear-view mirror at the car pressing up his backside.

He was proud of his firm, Gowan Partnerships: set it up in Toxon with his friend Pete Williams, not long after college. Pete didn't have any cash, but John had money from his inheritance so they used his name. They handled bigger clients as time went on; and now, they were well-known locally.

The countryside dispersed, and Toxon's first roundabout appeared with a line of traffic. The town was set in a valley, and its dirty streets reflected a pale spring sun that scattered deadweight over the town. Red brick slums oozed false pride onto the entrapped town centre. Those who earned enough fled to the far-reaching countryside in the early evening but retraced their steps the following morning. The tallest buildings stood dirty – grey stains stained by greyer stains – with concrete balconies and washing hanging out to dry. The odd care was taken, every six or so stories up, with potted flowers and clean windows.

He parked in the multi-storey and walked into the adjoining mall. People seemed unusual, chatting in small groups. He eyed the newspapers in the newsagents and was amazed by the headline:

'HUGE EXPLOSION AT ZENITH STAR
BUILDING – MANY FEARED DEAD'

Beneath the title, there was a photograph of police and debris, presumably in the middle of Blanworth, but the location was unrecognisable. He went to a café nearby, bought a cup of tea and read:

'Yesterday afternoon, at about 4.30 p.m., there was an enormous explosion at the Zenith Star Holdings plc building in the centre of Blanworth. Emergency services rushed to the scene, amid a spate of 999 calls, to find the building had collapsed. Many Zenith office workers, Zenith Star Security, employees of the building's high street shops, and members of the public are feared dead. The city's fire brigade is leading a major rescue operation. Relatives, friends and colleagues of the missing anxiously await news. Below is a hotline number for more information.

'The cause of the explosion is yet to be ascertained, but police are not ruling out the possibility it is terrorist related. Nobody has yet claimed responsibility. Gas engineers and fire department experts cannot begin their investigation until the rescue operation is completed and the building, or what is left of it, has been made safe.

'Graham Fielding was walking home from Murphy's pub on the High Street when he heard a tremendous explosion: "I've never heard anything like it before. I looked to my right and saw the Zenith building collapse in smoke." A fire department spokesman said that Mr Fielding was a very lucky man to escape injury from flying glass.

'Late last night, council workers cleared the public highway of glass and debris, and the road was reopened in time for this morning's rush hour traffic.'

The building had been one of those faceless, modern glass constructions that lacked humanity, John thought. Maybe a compassionate architect pushed the button!

Outside the shopping centre, life seemed pretty normal. The cobbled High Street was busy, and hooded teenagers swarmed the area before school, searching for intimidations and other destructive enjoyments. The church bell struck the hour, reliving its medieval fantasy. One shop window was boarded up from the weekend's 'festivities'.

Across the centre of town, John approached the building where he worked. It loomed above the others. Unfortunately, it was a throw up from the '60s' era, like the high-rise council flats elsewhere in town, but it was spacious and practical inside with a round reception desk in the centre of the foyer. Here, a well-groomed young man, with a designer beard, disliked the repetitive cold draft that flew through the electric doors and into his face. To the left were the lifts from where John's personal assistant, Janice, emerged.

'Heard the news?' she asked, holding a packet of cigarettes.

'Yes, terrible.'

She looked at him with the knowing look that he was being sarcastic as far as the building, itself, went, and she tucked one side of her auburn hair behind her ear before passing him. In the lift, he imagined the ugly Zenith building falling in slow motion to the ground and wondered whether he knew any of the fatalities. He didn't know any Zenith employees but had once bumped into the elusive CEO, Mr Wilkinson, at a Chamber of Commerce meeting.

In the Gowan Partnerships' office, a few employees turned and acknowledged him with smiles. Most desks had computers, others had drawing boards. The walls were white with framed posters of famous buildings, such as the Guggenheim Museum in Spain and The Portland Building in America. On the left side was a line of windows looking out onto Toxon. To the right were a couple of rooms including the private office of his business partner, Pete Williams, where John knocked and walked in.

Pete was sat at a desk with a large window behind him which displayed Toxon's hills, stacked with red houses. He had thick black-framed glasses, smartly combed hair to one side and a pink bow tie.

'I only just found out,' John said, sitting in front of the desk. The desk was made of bright plastic with three-dimensional tree grains and sensuously curved edges.

'I tried calling your mobile,' Pete said, in a low-pitched, nasal voice.

'I wonder what will go in its place.'

'Well, *we* certainly won't have anything to do with it. Some famous fuck will do it.'

'Nice to dream though.'

A few minutes later, John stood in his private office, located at the end of the main office, staring out of the window onto Toxon. The church in the centre of town stood defiantly, reaching up to God. But regardless of who or what it was for, John thought, *that* architect had had drive and passion for the building. John hadn't left his mark yet.

He left his office abruptly and stopped at Janice's desk: 'Cancel the meeting. Thought I might go and have a look at the wreckage, see what's happening and talk to some people. You never know, an opportunity may come our way.'

'Really?' Janice asked.

He felt embarrassed. Zenith Star Holdings was an international firm, and the destroyed building was its head office with high street shops on the ground floor. As Pete implied, it would be foolish to think *they* would be chosen for a project on such large prime real estate, but John couldn't help but dream.

Not far from his office was the dilapidated train station where he decided to go rather than taking the slower car journey. He waited impatiently on the platform before the old train screeched and let him on. It sliced through granite cliffs as it exited Toxon valley, continuing through rugged terrain for a couple of miles until the countryside became more placid, with distant cooling towers bellowing grey smoke in the distance.

He thought of the people in the building – one second, alive; the next, dead. It was tragic. But what did the future hold? Perhaps Zenith might allow anybody to compete for the contract… But there would be time for grieving first, of course.

The land flattened and dulled as Blanworth appeared. The station was bigger than Toxon's on account of Blanworth being a city, and it took a minute to walk to a taxi outside.

'Traffic bad today?' John asked as they drove out.

'Yes, mate, getting worse. Wait till the rest of the world's media gets here.'

They turned off the inner ring road, drove through the edge of a Muslim neighbourhood, with red brick terraced houses, and progressed towards the heart of the city, where the buildings became whiter and larger. The cab stopped at the bottom of the High Street.

Blanworth City Centre was cleaner and tidier than Toxon but more fake, lying about its true nature which lay in the surrounding council estates. There were gentrified areas too, like the golf course and yachting lake, but all computer-generated and adding to the sense of fakery and claustrophobia. The council decided whether a tree, bush or park was tamed enough. The council decided whether a man could build an extension on his house. The council decided whether a proposed building was too tall. And the city's wildlife embraced it from a loser's standpoint. Pigeons were obtrusive, insects were dutiful and people were both. The local newspaper encouraged the reader to believe that the football team was doing better. Every season they were either at the top of one league or the bottom of the other, with the club's owner taking handsome profits for himself, selling off the only good players, and laughing. He was a character, and a character is admired. And yet, thought John, the explosion showed a glimmer of hope…

He walked up the High Street toward a crowd of people in City Square. On the other side of the Square, there was no building, just a pile of outstretching rubble and diagonal shafts of metal that towered above the crowd. People seemed more exhilarated than mournful, taking videos with phones and professional cameras. Police had cordoned off the area. There were several fire engines and numerous police cars. The eastern sun, thinly veiled by clouds, hovered in the skyline's gap.

No buildings had been connected to the Zenith building,

but the High Street in front of it was full of debris with ravaged shop buildings on the other side: walls were caved in; rooms were laid bare; and any red-tiled roofs that remained were lopsided. On the right side of what used to be the Zenith building, the nearest structure was largely unaffected with only a few broken windows overlooking the side road that separated them.

John passed a dishevelled tramp, sitting on a bench, and tried talking to a stranger at the back of the crowd: 'Have they recovered any bodies?'

'Several.'

John pushed through the crowd for a while, towards the front. There had to be at least four hundred people here. He made it to the police tape. A couple of firemen were leaning against a fire engine and drinking bottles of water.

'Gruesome work,' John shouted.

They remained silent and looked elsewhere.

John stood in awe of the rubble where a building had stood for practically his entire life, before moving out of the crowd again.

'Do you have a cigarette, sir?' a voice said to his side, the accent faintly Scottish.

John turned and saw the tramp staring up from his bench. He was famous in the city. Legend had it that he used to be a wealthy reporter, working in London, but couldn't handle the pressure so adopted this lifestyle. Probably bullshit. He grabbed a cigarette from John with crimson fingernails and eagerly inhaled from John's lighter.

'Were you anywhere near here last night?' John asked.

'Sitting right here.'

'You saw everything, then!'

'Aye, a big bang.'

'Maybe for the best – quite an ugly building.'

The tramp stared emotionlessly at him, and John walked away before turning back to take a final look at the rubble.

2

A few days later, John looked through the bedroom window to the distant gate at the top of the driveway, wondering whether the newspaper had yet been delivered. Information released earlier this week had described a long wheelbase Ford Transit Van gaining access to the Zenith, underground car park, presumably duping the security guards in the process. Miraculously preserved CCTV footage showed a man of dark complexion, sporting sunglasses and wearing blue overalls, walking quickly away from the car park entrance three minutes before the car bomb rendered the building history. A terrorist group from North Africa had claimed responsibility for the attack, and a massive manhunt was underway across Europe for five British men.

158 bodies had been recovered; twenty-three people were still missing; three survivors had been found and were expected to make a full recovery; and neither the Zenith Chairman, Mr Wilkinson, nor his employee son, Mr Wilkinson Junior, was in the building at the time.

Zenith was a wholesale clothing company which supplied clothes around the world, including a contract with the Israeli Defence Forces for military clothing. On a business trip to Israel last year, the Chairman's son had made disparaging remarks about Muslims wanting to take back land from the Israelis. He later apologised, but his comments went public.

Robust television coverage asked endless leading questions put a hundred different ways to 'experts'. The Prime Minister sounded confident as he patronised and implored the general public to 'Carry on as usual'.

Downstairs in the kitchen, John made breakfast. The kitchen had been the most expensive room in the house with tiled flooring, marble work surfaces and an impressive AGA cooker. The wife had wanted her mod con kitchen, but there were far too many appliances, even for three people in the house, and now many of them were derelict and dusty.

Leaving an egg in the frying pan, John walked up the long, bendy driveway to the gate. The wind was strong away from the house, and the conifer trees on the perimeter of his land rustled like waving hands. Farmers' fields stretched beyond. He opened the back of the letterbox, which was housed inside the right gate pillar, and took out the newspaper:

'ZENITH STAR SHARES SUSPENDED

'Just as we were going to press on Thursday morning, shares in Zenith Star Holdings plc, listed on the AIM market, were suspended following a collapse in the share price precipitated by the terrorist outrage on the company's principal asset. A statement was subsequently released to the LSE. (See "Company Comment" on page 3.)'

John turned to page 3:

'The destroyed Head Office of Zenith Star Holdings plc, its principle asset, occupies a prime commercial site of half an acre in the centre of the City of Blanworth. The company joined the AIM market six months prior to the attack, exuding confidence that recent events have dispelled. A statement to the LSE confirmed that Zenith's insurance cover for acts of terrorism had not been renewed. In an interview with the Chairman, our financial reporter was informed that the decision to exclude terrorism had been taken at the previous Board meeting, as part of a policy to trim costs – a fateful decision indeed! It now remains to be seen what can be salvaged from this tragedy. As the principle creditors are a banking consortium, the final outcome could well be a debt for equity swap, leaving private investors owning little or nothing of the company.'

With the news that Zenith wasn't insured for terrorism, and the fact that the Zenith building was their principle asset, it seemed unlikely Zenith would construct a new building. But somebody would: the site was too valuable to remain unoccupied for long.

Two weeks later, on a Sunday evening, having gone into the office only a couple of times since the attack, John sat in the cosy lamplight of his study, situated at the top/back of the house. The oak pedestal desk, positioned in front of the window, looked out onto a gently descending lawn. On the desk was a green lamp, and by its side stood an antique drawing board, made of oak with cast iron legs, and a matching wooden stool. He worked in his study far more than he did at the office, designing garages, small blocks of flats for the council and occasionally more fulfilling projects, such as an imitation of a Roman bath house with modern comforts.

Also on the desk was an open bottle of whisky that had scented the room overnight. Beside it were scribbled notes about designing the new Zenith building:

'...am I mad? How could I ever, even hope to be the designer of the new Zenith building in the heart of Blanworth? I've never designed anything remotely the size, and I'm just a local architect, nothing compared to the bigger names. And yet, I feel something I haven't felt for a long time. The atmosphere, the very nature of things has changed. The buildings, the people, the sky...'

He felt inspired by his drunken ramblings and thought of the new building that could fill the old site. Couldn't he go to the site tonight, take measurements and get more of a sense of it? His mobile rang abruptly.

'Hi, Janice, what's up?' he said.

'You haven't been in much for the past few weeks. Just wondering if everything is okay?'

'Fine. You know it's Sunday, don't you?'

'Are you still thinking of the Zenith building?'

'A bit,' he said, knowing how ludicrous it seemed to her –

wishing to design the next building. 'Anyway, Janice, nice of you to ring. Got to get on with something.'

'You in tomorrow?'

She was either worried about him, keen on him or both. Probably the former.

'Maybe.'

He collected his notepad and then his torch from a kitchen cupboard, went outside to the garage, which was a few metres to the side of the house, and drove his Jaguar into the spring dusk. The stars were beginning to shine, and a new moon hovered low in the sky. He accelerated through the iron gates at the top of the driveway and along the medieval road which meandered through ancient woodlands and land holdings.

What did the site look like now? Much of the rubble was probably cleared in the search for survivors, but it would still be cordoned off by police tape. The search for any more survivors had been exhausted.

Dark woods gave way to dark farmers' fields; and eventually, he approached the main road to turn left to Blanworth for a few miles. The approach into Blanworth was flat. Buildings lit the night, particularly the cathedral with its numerous spires and central tower. He parked on the roofless top of the multi-storey and stood next to the low wall protecting him from a bus lane far below. To one side was the adjoining Princegate Shopping Centre, and to the other was the east side of the city. Could he leave a legacy in this town, the town he grew up in?

He moved quickly through the shopping centre, passing the odd person and unlit shops, and out through the doors into City Square. A wind blew into his face, as if suddenly the new gap on the other side of the Square had relieved a pressure. Much of the debris in the surrounding area had been cleared over the two and a half weeks, leaving a thin slither of public access down the High Street next to ravaged, old shop buildings where apparently some pedestrians had died. On the site, itself, there was now a lower level of rubble. Unmanned trucks were parked idly by the side, and dormant cranes hovered above. John couldn't see any workers and hoped the clear-up process had finished for today.

Tonight's exercise was technically pointless, because all the information he needed about the site was on the Internet, but he wanted to feel the ground with his own 'two hands'. He approached the tramp in the same place on the bench and prodded a dirty leg with his torch: 'Don't mind if I take a look, do you?'

The tramp's lifeless eyes opened, and John walked on. With the torch shining, he stepped over the police tape and scrambled over stones whilst avoiding twisted shafts of steel. The feeling of cold concrete on the skin of his hand felt good, but it was strange to think that people died here.

'You there!' a policeman shouted, and John lost his balance several times as he approached the policeman. John explained he was an architect, but the policeman told him it was very dangerous and allowed him only to walk just outside the perimeter for five minutes. It was all John needed anyway.

He counted his strides and began to feel more in tune with the site, as if he were a part of it.

Back at the bench, he angled the notepad to the lamp post light and wrote the following:

'My perimeter walk:
Length: 60 metres
Width: 55 metres'

He made a rough calculation to determine how much wider the perimeter of the cordoned off area was to the original perimeter of the building.

'News people were here,' the tramp said. 'Caught you on camera.'

John couldn't see any news people or anybody else, for that matter. 'How long for?'

'A few minutes, until the police came.'

Back on Blanworth Road a mile out of the city, John parked in the brightly lit petrol station and filled up his Jag. A bored girl behind the till served him. Her apathy and lack of make-up, attractive. She reminded him of his daughter. He threw his pack of cigs on the passenger seat and drove out without strapping himself in.

It was raining hard. The tarmac was smooth and straight. He passed a sign that said twenty-six miles to Toxon and drove for several minutes at increasing speed before turning onto the rougher, snake-like road that led directly to his house.

He sped around corners, slowing down initially but

turning at, and accelerating to, dangerous speeds. The vast, dark countryside pervaded the periphery of his vision, and the crystal grey road appeared bright and intense. Lights from an approaching car blinded him as it passed, and he swerved quickly to realign himself. He felt the excitement of life growing inside him, and the dark fields and road seemed to unite with his experience into one fiery ball of energy. It was the culmination of the past couple of weeks – the destruction of the old building, the worldwide media attention and the prospect of a new building to take its place – that seemed to explode into this moment. And with it came an unadulterated confidence that he would be the architect of the new Blanworth building! He approached another corner far too quickly and hit the brake as he began to move the steering wheel to the right, but the car suddenly began to spin in a whoosh, and he felt it descend off the road into a ditch as his head hit the steering wheel.

3

John awoke in darkness. There were noises: squeaks on the floor, like trainers rubbing against a shiny surface, and the sound of female voices: 'Bring her through here,' one said. There was a sharp, unnatural smell of disinfectant too, and he realised he was in hospital.

He remembered last night clearly: he'd been at the site in Blanworth, taking measurements; he'd driven home afterwards, increasing his speed as he thought about being the next architect; and then he'd crashed into the bend. Idiot! Idiot for two reasons: one, he had crashed his car; and two, in his excitement he had believed he was going to be the architect of the next building! It must have been the night air or something.

There was a noise of clothes rustling and general body movement, this time much closer to him. Suddenly, an unbearable, bright light appeared, and he instinctively closed his eyes with a hard pull of his facial muscles.

'Mr Gowan?' a male voice asked.

John opened his eyes tentatively. The light was easier this time and less painful, and he realised he was looking up at a man with brown skin and glasses, looking down at him.

'Hello,' John said.

'How are you feeling?'

The man's face was a little too close to focus easily, so John looked away towards the blue curtains with flowery patterns that surrounded the bed. For the first time, he realised his forehead was throbbing a little, though not much. Again, he remembered crashing into the bend and even hitting his head onto the steering wheel.

'I'm feeling okay, I think. I think I hit my head, right? Concussion or something?'

'That's right, Mr Gowan,' the man said, with an Indian accent.

John looked back at him. He had large eyes. He was dressed in a white coat and had a stethoscope around his neck.

'How do you know my name?' John said. 'Did you look in my wallet?'

The doctor shook his head. 'Of course I know your name. You remember telling me last night, don't you?'

John didn't remember anything, but a fear of exposing his vulnerability, when already in such a vulnerable position, made him lie instinctively: 'Oh, yes.'

'And you remember the CT scan?'

John nodded.

'Good,' the doctor said. 'As I said last night, you have bruising to your head, but nothing at all to worry about, not as long as you rest. I'd like to keep you in for just another day, and then you shouldn't work for at least a couple of days – just take it easy.'

John closed his eyes and tried remembering more details from last night after he had hit his head but couldn't remember anything new. All he saw was darkness. He opened his eyes again.

'I know, I know,' the doctor said. 'I know that you'll want to get to work today with everything that's going on, but you simply can't.' He waved his finger and opened his eyes wide: 'Strict orders from your Doctor Patel, okay?'

John nodded slowly, wondering why the hell the doctor was speaking to him in such a familiar way. Why would the doctor believe that John would want to go to work today? And why couldn't John remember anything from the hospital last night?

'I would like you to do something for me,' the doctor said. He bent down to a chair beside the bed and unearthed a newspaper from John's jacket which hung on the back of the chair. John couldn't remember having had a newspaper last night. Also on the chair were the rest of his clothes laid neatly: his blue sweater, trousers, pants and socks. For the first time he realised he was wearing a pale blue hospital gown with nothing underneath.

The doctor waved the newspaper in front of him: 'I want you to read the newspaper to me, just a paragraph.'

John looked at the newspaper in the doctor's hands: 'Is that my newspaper?'

The doc smiled and nodded: 'Will you read it?'

John felt a pain in his forehead and raised his hand towards it. The skin was sore from where he had hit his head on the steering wheel. He remembered the petrol station before he crashed and guessed he must have bought the newspaper there.

'Mr Gowan, are you okay?'

'I'm fine, just a little head pain.'

'Don't worry, that's to be expected, and you're in good hands. If it gets worse, then tell me or a nurse.' He glanced down at the newspaper: 'So will you read it?'

'Why do I have to read it?'

'Because sometimes it is difficult to read after a concussion, and I want to see how well you are. But also, I would very much like to keep it, if you don't mind, and ask you to sign it, if you please. I feel very honoured to have you as my patient.' His eyes widened further, and he smiled even more.

Who the hell was this nut? In addition to not remembering the newspaper from last night, John had a weirdo for a doctor to contend with. He would do as the doctor asked him, though, and then hopefully he would go away. Tentatively, he took the newspaper from the doctor's hands.

'I need my glasses,' John said. 'They're probably in my trouser pocket.'

The doctor bent down, unearthed his thin green glasses case from a trouser pocket and handed it to him. John looked down at the newspaper and read aloud:

'In court number one at the Old Bailey this morning, the five defendants, found guilty on all counts of the terrorist attack on the Blanworth office building which resulted in the death of 181 people, were sentenced by Judge Richards.

They all received life sentences, with the recommendation that they serve a minimum of thirty-five years each before being considered for parole, except for the mastermind, Abdulla Hussain, who received a recommended minimum of forty years.'

There was a picture of Abdulla Hussain, dressed in a dark suit, next to the article. John was immediately confused. Since when were the terrorists captured? Not only captured, but sentenced? All this took time. John saw the News on television yesterday, and nothing like this had happened. What was wrong with this place, the weird doctor, the newspaper that didn't make any sense? Was he still dreaming?

'What the hell is this?' John blurted.

The doctor looked bemused, and his fingers fiddled with his stethoscope which hung around his neck: 'Is there a problem? You can certainly read well. Your eyes seem to be fine.'

'Are you a real doctor? Aren't you supposed to look into my eyes with a light or something?'

'We checked you last night, Mr Gowan.'

'So, then, what about this newspaper?' John looked down at the title: 'Blanworth Express'. This was the normal local paper alright, but what the hell was this article! He glanced elsewhere on the page, looking for something that might give him an answer. Date: 'October 28th [Year]' John froze. The date on the newspaper was not the real date. The real date was March 15th [Year] – three years earlier. John looked up at him: 'What the hell!'

'What's wrong, Mr Gowan?'

'What's going on? The date on the newspaper says…'

'What date do you think it is?'

It had to be a typing error, a misprint: 'The date on the newspaper says October 28th [Year].'

The doctor nodded: 'Is there anything wrong? Don't forget that's yesterday's newspaper, so it's yesterday's date. What date do you think it is? Please don't be alarmed if you're a couple of days out. You have concussion and that's perfectly normal.'

A couple of days out! This loon and this newspaper were saying it was three and a half years in the fucking future!

'I…'

John felt very afraid. Both the newspaper and the doctor couldn't be wrong. He closed his eyes and tried understanding what was happening to him. He needed time to think. He needed space on his own. What the hell was happening? Was he living in the future? How could that be? With immense effort, he tried to be calm and show the doctor that he was fine, just so that he would go away and John could think.

'I'm fine, actually,' he said, opening his eyes.

'What date do you think it is?' the doctor repeated.

With as much composure as John could muster, he said: 'It's yesterday's newspaper, so today's date must be October 29 th , of course.'

The doctor stared at him a moment, clearly unconvinced, but then a smile suddenly beamed across his face: 'Oh, I understand. It's only now you've remembered the importance of this morning, is it? You want to get out of here and back to the site, do you?'

The doctor was now saying something else that didn't make sense. John couldn't take any more; the confusion of the moment was too overwhelming: 'Please, I just think I need some rest.'

'Good idea! I'll get the nurse to pull the curtains and perhaps bring you some food and drink. Would you like that?'

'Sure.'

'But I can't have you going to the site today. You need rest. There is no way I'm letting the great John Gowan go to the Zenith site. What do you think would happen to me if I said you were fit to go the day after concussion? The press would destroy me! I'd lose my job, my reputation! We can't have that, now can we!' The doctor cackled and his white teeth gleamed demonically.

'No…' John said, trying hard not to think or question what the doctor was saying from sheer fear. 'We can't have that.'

The doctor thrust a pen in front of John's face: 'Please, though, if you don't want to keep the newspaper, sign it before you go.'

'What?'

'Oh please, it would be for my son, you see. He's crazy about the new Zenith building.'

What the hell…? What new Zenith building? John's mind raced, trying to piece together the facts: he had wanted to design the next Zenith building in the moments before he crashed his car; he was now living three and a half years in the future; and the doctor wanted him to sign a newspaper about a new Zenith building. Was John the new Zenith architect? Had he really gone on to design the next Zenith building, and had Zenith accepted his designs?

'So, will you sign the newspaper for me? It would be great, because nearly all of this newspaper is dedicated to your building, as you will know, including the terrorist story which is linked, of course.' He paused and sighed. 'Poetic justice, isn't it, that they were sentenced yesterday, the day before construction began? I think you're on page 4 and 5, a double spread.'

John couldn't believe what he was hearing. It was all too much. He could hardly breathe. His heart raced whilst his body stiffened with shock, which was probably why he looked normal to the doctor.

'Please, I just need a little space,' John said, with a voice barely audible. 'Can you leave it with me?'

The doctor sighed. 'Okay then, but I expect it to be signed by the time I come back!' With that, the doctor smiled, turned and walked away through the small gap in the curtains.

Frantic images of the speeding road last night appeared to him. It suddenly seemed a mystical experience: being sure of becoming the next architect, crashing his car in his excitement and waking up three and a half years later to learn he *was* the new architect. It was the perfect elapse of time from deciding to become the next architect and crashing his car, to waking up on the first day of construction, having designed the building. What was happening? Why was it happening? Was he dreaming? He hurriedly swiped the pages open to page 5.

A picture of him smiling serenely with sunglasses was on the page next to the caption: 'The Freedom Building'. Beneath, it read:

'Three and a half years ago, after the destruction of the old Zenith Star building, the little-known architect John Gowan had a dream to design a new building that might not only restore Blanworth's city skyline but revolutionise it. With only this dream and with fierce competition from across the globe, he designed a building that Zenith immediately accepted. In a recent interview for this newspaper, Mr Wilkinson the CEO of Zenith said:

"When I saw the design of Mr Gowan's new building, I immediately knew that this would be it. It was so different to any building I had ever seen in my life. Its innovation, its grandeur, its sheer audacity was thrilling to me. All I needed was the council's and shareholders' approval to put this dream into action!"

And, indeed, Mr Wilkinson was allowed to put his dream into action. With the approval of everybody, Mr Wilkinson didn't wait long to get moving on the project. Here's Mr Gowan speaking last year:

"I'm very pleased with the speed at which things

are happening. There is a popular will to make it happen. It's almost like the early days of architecture when there was far less red tape. Construction will begin next year."'

John was impatient to see the design of the building, so he stopped reading and flicked to pages 2 and 3. On page 3 were lines of an object that cut into a bluish, cloudy sky, and he ascertained that it was a computer-generated picture of the future Zenith building, but his vision immediately began to blur as he looked at the picture. He tried tensing his eyes to see it; but the harder he tried, the more he seemed to lose a sense of what he was looking at and, indeed, what he was doing. The headache, emanating from his forehead, became worse too, and he felt his blood pumping into the area above his nose. He closed his eyes, let go of the newspaper and consoled himself with the thought that he would look at the building later – after he had rested. The day was overwhelming, and he suddenly began to feel faint.

He awoke to find the curtains drawn back to the wall, revealing a large room. A few people in beds along the opposite wall and on his side were looking at him. In the centre of the room was an aisle where nurses walked. By the side of his bed was a trolley with food. John wondered whether the meeting with the doctor was a dream. Were people staring at him on this ward because he appeared odd to them, and not because he was the new Zenith architect? A nurse passed and John lifted his hand: 'Nurse!'

She stopped and turned. She was thin, tall and middle aged: 'Yes, Mr Gowan?'

'How do you know me?

She appeared concerned and walked to the bed: 'You're Mr Gowan, architect of the Zenith building. Are you feeling okay?'

John froze for a moment, then mustered the words: 'Yes, I'm fine.'

She smiled and walked away.

One of the people staring at him was an old man sitting opposite, so John turned to evade the stare, only to see other people glancing at him, too. He moved himself into a more defensive position, rising to an upright posture and putting the pillow behind his back. He closed his eyes and tried remembering the past few years. A formless darkness confronted him. The lack of memory was formidable, and the fear became a little too intense, so he opened his eyes. His forehead throbbed. He put his hand to his head, wondering how he could have crashed last night and hit his head on the steering wheel, if last night wasn't last night.

The nurse appeared again: 'There is a Janice Stephens waiting outside for you, claiming to be your personal assistant. Would you like to see her? There was also the press, but I sent them away.'

He suddenly felt warm and jubilant. Janice was somebody with whom he could feel comfortable telling the truth to get answers: 'Janice! Yes, please, send her in.'

'Would you also like to eat your meal now?'

'Yes, please, after I've seen Janice.'

Moments later, Janice appeared from a few beds down, walking towards him. She looked like the same old Janice: auburn hair down to her shoulders, blue jeans, smart woolly jumper and a knowing smile on her lips. She walked up to John and kissed him on the side of the head.

'What have you gone and done, then?' she said.

John was surprised at the delicate kiss and felt a great warmth flood his heart: he needed the familiarity, the warmth, the end of loneliness. Janice retracted her face a little and looked at him.

'Are you okay?' she said, after a moment of staring at each other.

John nodded hurriedly: 'Please, take a seat.'

She put the glasses case and newspaper onto the floor and manoeuvred the chair to face him: 'I hope you don't mind me sitting on your clothes.'

'Tell me, Janice, have you heard exactly what happened to me last night?'

'Yes, I have.'

'What have you heard?'

'That you were at the site, fell and hit your head.'

Finally, he had an explanation for his head injury, if crashing his car hadn't happened last night. But her explanation seemed very weird, his not being able to remember: 'At the site?'

'Don't you remember?'

'Oh, yes, I remember being at the site,' he said, wanting to hide his amnesia from her until he knew all the facts, 'but I don't remember falling and hitting my head. The doctor said slight amnesia is perfectly normal after concussion. Do you know anything more about what happened to me?'

'Just that the tramp came to your rescue.'

'The tramp?'

'Didn't they tell you?'

John knew Janice would deduce he had extensive amnesia very soon, but his questions did not reveal it yet: 'No, please tell me.'

'Oh. Well apparently, you had left your phone on the bench in the Square, and the tramp walked onto the site to give it to you. You'd left the gate to the site open, so he walked through and found you there – this is what he told paramedics, at least.'

John remembered sitting with the tramp on the bench last night, then walking onto the site – but last night wasn't last night: 'Okay, then what?'

'He used your phone to call for the ambulance.'

John remained still and tried to give a normal answer: 'That was good of him.'

'Yes, otherwise you would probably have awoken at the site on your own with terrible concussion.'

He looked at Janice and was ready to tell her everything, but he noticed shallow cracks around her eyes which never used to be so pronounced. The roots of her hair, too, showed stark grey. Fear overcame him, and he realised she was not the Janice he knew three and a half years ago: she was a Janice allied to this future world. The throbbing in his forehead became a little more intense as he also realised he needed to be guarded and defensive, until he knew exactly how and why he had massive amnesia. He composed himself.

'Are you okay?' Janice said. She, like the newspaper, like the crazy doctor, like the strange people in the ward, who were systematically glancing at him, and like the formidable darkness he witnessed when closing his eyes, trying to remember the previous three and a half years, was alien to him. How could he possibly tell her the truth – a person allied to these alien experiences?

'Just fine,' he said.

4

The next day after breakfast, Janice arrived wearing jeans and an auburn jumper that matched her hair. The lines around her eyes weren't so noticeable with more make-up. The doctor had warned John not to work this week but to get some rest and organise an appointment with his GP in a day or two, to make sure everything was okay.

On John's same old phone there were a few new contacts such as 'Mann' and 'Andrew' – names he didn't recognise – and in his call register there was no record of any calls except the 999 call the tramp must have made two nights ago. John would have to thank him.

Wearing his own clothes, he walked with Janice out of the hospital into the warm glare of sunlight and smiled. He felt sure that he would remember everything soon; but meanwhile, he could look upon the world with curiosity and observe the changes of three and a half years.

'Mr Gowan?' a male voice said.

He turned with Janice. A man with thin black hair, slightly hunched shoulders and a navy-blue suit approached.

'Hello, I'm Detective Murphy.' He flashed them his identity card. 'I just called the hospital to see whether you were still here. Apologies that I couldn't see you sooner. I wanted to ask you whether you remembered anything from Sunday night – the night you fell?'

John still recalled nothing, but he had to say something: 'I can remember walking onto the site, but that's as far as it goes.'

'Do you remember anybody following you or acting suspicious?'

Murphy glanced uneasily at Janice.

'She's my long-standing PA,' John said. 'We have no secrets. But no, I think I just fell as the doctor said.'

The detective looked at John's forehead: 'So the mark on your head was caused by a fall, rather than somebody hitting you on the head?'

'Sure.'

'So why didn't you put your hands out when you fell?'

'I suppose they were in my pockets, and I didn't have time.'

The detective nodded: 'Okay. If you're not suspicious of your being hit, and the doctor isn't either, then there won't be any need for me to question the homeless man who, as I understand, called the ambulance for you. I just wanted to make sure that you were sure. If you even hinted to a reporter that you might have been hit, then things in this city could turn ugly – very fast.'

'Why's that?'

'You are the architect of the building that replaces the old one destroyed by terrorists. If there was even speculation that a Muslim hit you, we might get a repeat of the race riots we had a couple of years ago – the white backlash after the destruction of the old Zenith building.'

Learning this information quickly, John pretended he remembered and nodded the best he could: 'I'll tell anybody who asks me, I believe I fell.'

'But if you do remember something that might indicate someone hit you,' the detective said, holding a card, 'then call me first.'

They left the detective, and Janice drove out of the hospital car park and along the road until they approached a T junction where she flicked the right-hand indicator.

'We need to go left,' John said.

'We're going back to your house, John.'

He'd been waiting until now to tell her they were going to the Zenith site. He didn't dare tell her in hospital near the doctor, or the doctor would never have let him leave. He needed to see the site three and a half years later, having seemingly only just come from it when it was still full of debris on the night he crashed his car. He needed to see the change in all that time and whether it might jog his memory.

'We need to go to the site. I need to have a word with Pete about something.' Pete had rung the hospital that morning whilst John was asleep, with the reassuring message that he would take John's place as the resident architect.

'But the doctor told you not to work.'

A car beeped behind them.

'I won't be working,' he said. 'Pete's doing my job today, and I just want a word with him. Is that so much to ask?'

She remained still a moment. The car behind beeped

again. She sighed and turned left.

It was autumn now, unlike the spring to which he was accustomed, with falling leaves from trees that overhung the road on the approach to the city centre. Cars appeared different, with Fords and Saabs having sleeker edges and niftier headlights. But there was the other change, too: not so obvious but pervading all of reality in a way he couldn't quite describe. He knew he was living in the future and that the problem of his memory lay with him – not the world around him. Knowing all this, however, couldn't overcome the visual impression that it was reality that seemed to have changed, distorting the look of the clouds, the cars and the people. Everything appeared otherworldly. Nevertheless, soon he would integrate with this future world when his memories returned and become the Zenith architect, his true self.

They ascended the bridge that went over the railway, and Blanworth's City Centre appeared. The cathedral towered above all other buildings despite it being further away, and the gap in the skyline, where the Zenith building used to be, appeared stark with only tall, thin cranes in its place. At the bottom of the bridge, they continued straight onto the road that led directly to City Square and the site.

At the corner of City Square, they turned with the road and drove down the side road, with the site beside them to the left. It was surrounded by eight-foot-high, wooden hoarding which wasn't there the last time that John remembered being here. They stopped at the entrance. The golden morning sun streamed across a muddy expanse as builders in yellow hats walked or stood, shouting to each other while drinking cups of tea. John watched in awe, feeling a strange sense of pride that everything here was following the designs which he couldn't remember creating.

'What now?' Janice said.

A horn sound blasted behind them. The tyres of a large truck pressed into the rear-view mirror, wanting to get onto the site.

'Go!' John said.

'Onto the site?'

'No! Just forwards.'

She did so, a little way, and John got out. 'Just park in the car park, keep your phone on you and I'll see you very soon.'

She looked at him with a reluctant expression that said: 'You've just come out of hospital and the doctor told you not to do any work.'

He entered the site. Trucks, diggers, cranes and workmen continually moved into different arrangements and positions. If he had witnessed an otherworldly environment since leaving the hospital, then it was nothing compared to this. Everything here had vastly changed from the rubble and debris that he saw in what seemed like only two nights ago, and he visualised how he must have walked here and planned on this site many times in the intervening three and a half years. He had a past here as his true self – the designer of the new building – and he was sure to have a future here, too. But so far, no memories.

'Mr Gowan?' someone shouted, over explosive sounds

of hydraulics and grinding metal that resembled wounded elephants in the final stages of life.

John smiled confidently, acting like his true self, and was given a yellow hard hat. He asked for the whereabouts of Pete Williams, and the workman pointed to a green Portakabin at the front of the site, with City Square behind it.

This morning, when he had woken, John had looked for the newspaper with the picture designs of the building but someone had taken it. There would undoubtedly be blueprints of the building inside the Portakabin which would surely spark his memory. With a pounding heart, John walked along the edge of the hoarding, climbed the two small wooden steps and pushed through the door.

Coats hung on the wall directly in front of him, and as he turned he saw a large A2 sheet with a timetable, presumably displaying the construction schedule, then a sink and a table against the wall. Sitting at the table facing John was a man with a colourful shirt, a side parting and thick black-rimmed glasses. It was Pete. He looked the same as he always did, at least from this distance. Sitting near him was a short but broad man with a beard and balding head. John didn't recognise him.

'You're out,' Pete said, in his distinctively low-pitched, nasal voice.

John grinned confidently.

'Hello, John,' the other man said.

John kept the smile and pretended to recognise him: 'How are things going?'

42

The man nodded: 'Like clockwork. The first day and a half have gone well.'

'Sorry I didn't come and see you, John.' Pete patted his hair gently: an odd mannerism of his which three and a half years hadn't changed. 'But I thought you'd want me here, instead.'

John nodded, walked to the table and glanced down to see what they were looking at. The papers appeared to be building plans, but he couldn't decipher their details, upside down. In a few moments, he would see them the correct way up and at last know the basic appearance of the building. What did the building that the newspaper had been praising as a work of genius actually look like? With a sudden rush of excitement, he walked around the table and sat between them in front of the plans.

'Did you fall, or did somebody hit you?' the man said.

'I fell,' John said, adjusting his seat, and ready now to look down at his building designs. Surely, he would recognise them, and his memories would come flooding back.

Pete pressed his finger into them: 'We've been going over this week's schedule and looking at these blueprints.'

John leaned forward and looked at the paper. Vertical lines stretched down the page where they joined horizontal lines that stretched to the side of the page. In the centre were clusters of squares and rectangles interlinked and branching off in different directions. John looked at the title at the top of the page to understand what he was looking at. It said, 'FRONT ELEVATION.'

He looked back at the drawing and tried to see the picture as a whole. He tried to unify the vertical and horizontal lines, but he began to experience a similar problem to yesterday when he tried looking at the building in the newspaper. The lines seemed to divide into twos, bending in outward curves, and the white on the page became more prominent as the dark lines became weaker. He blinked and looked away to try to gain proper focus again. Perhaps, like yesterday, he was still too ill to be working, just as the doctor had said. Nevertheless, John felt a strong desire to see the building, and it had been a couple of days since the concussion. He looked back at the sheet.

The lines threatened to divide into twos again, and the shapes appeared ugly, not seeming to integrate properly with each other. The drawing seemed to be a confused mess of ugly lines and angles which were not coordinated in any way. What was he trying to look at?

'Looks like he can't believe he designed it, himself,' the man with the beard said.

John tried straining his eyes more to gain control over the image, but the drawing became even more contorted. The lines began to clump together and move clockwise. What was happening? Where was the building he was supposed to be looking at? The lines continued to move into a swirling mass. And at their heart, a pinprick of darkness began to grow – bigger and bigger. All of a sudden, he felt a pull from it as if it had the power of a black hole, and its size threatened to engulf the paper, sucking him and his consciousness into it. It had the same toneless tone, the same distinct impenetrable bleakness, as when he closed his eyes and tried to remember the design process. With as much strength as he could muster in his legs, feet and neck muscles, he turned and looked away. The dizzying darkness immediately exited his view, and he no longer felt its pull.

'John, are you okay?' Pete said, staring concernedly at him.

John realised he was panting, and he fought to regain his breath: 'I'm…' Was he okay? What had just happened? With trepidation, he turned back to the plans without looking at them directly. The swirling, black nothingness had disappeared.

He needed reflection, time to think. He had to get away: 'I'm feeling a bit dizzy. The doctor told me not to work. I shouldn't really be here.'

The journey home was odd and unsettling. Flat, fallow farmers' fields stretched toward distant lines of trees and appeared different to the fields he was used to seeing. 'A mild autumnal day', they were calling it on the radio.

They pulled into the petrol station: the same one John had used ten minutes before he crashed. As Janice left the car, he strained his eyes to see if the same apathetic, teenage girl was there, behind the counter. He couldn't see her, and she would be older now, anyway, perhaps even unrecognisable as a woman. He bit his thumb hard into the crease between the nail and the skin until it started to bleed.

A couple of miles onward, Janice turned off Blanworth Road and onto the road that led directly to John's house. It snaked through the countryside for miles whilst memories of that night – of headlights on the road and the bend approaching fast – returned to him. As Janice slowed to the bend, he remembered the feelings of elation and confidence for the future, of being absolutely sure that he would become the architect of the new Zenith building. He remembered the car suddenly swirling and the dizziness he felt as it left the road, crashing into the ditch.

The memory of crashing and of hitting his head against the steering wheel was mysterious, otherworldly . Did it really happen? And was he really here now, remembering it from three and a half years in the future? Had he really become the architect of the Zenith building? The muddy verge approximately where he crashed passed by, and as Janice accelerated from the bend his throat contracted with sickness.

The sky grew darker as they stopped outside the front gates of his place. The vertical, spear-like bars pointed towards the dark, heavy clouds with readiness as the gates opened automatically. Once inside, John got out of the car into the blustery gale and opened the postbox housed in the back of one of the gate pillars. There were a couple of letters, and he stood there without opening them or doing anything.

'Getting in?' Janice asked through the open window.

He stared at her and noticed the same cracks at the edges of her eyes that he saw yesterday in hospital. Today's make-up was fading.

'No, I'll walk down.'

'Are you okay, John?'

He widened his mouth into a smile.

She drove down the driveway which wound like a descending snake towards his house 120 metres away. It was the same as it always looked with its slate roof, dormer windows and symmetrically proportioned lower windows set in a wall of grey brick – the wife's choice with the council's permission, not John's. He had wanted something more exciting. But his unease with the house was not the wife's fault in this moment. There seemed something odd about it, something strange, set deeply as it was into the countryside landscape.

He walked directly to the house across the grass. The garden was encircled by a perimeter of conifers, a little taller now, and the garage appeared the same with a small path between it and the house. Behind the house the garden led down to the ancient, small wood at the bottom; and here, a change really had occurred: the oaks and beaches were decorated with autumnal reds and oranges instead of the stark winter branches to which he was accustomed. The wood disappeared from view as he approached Janice who stood beneath the porch, smoking a cigarette.

'Cigarettes!' he blurted, seizing the joy and having forgotten to get a packet at the petrol station. Remarkably, he hadn't thought about smoking since leaving the hospital.

She looked at him oddly, her auburn hair swirling at the edges. Why was she looking at him inquisitively? Had he done something to make her suspect his amnesia?

'You've started again?' she asked.

He realised his mistake but quickly lit one of her cigarettes, smiling as he did so, hoping that his smile and, therefore, his words appeared to mean that he belittled his possibly recent attempt to stop smoking. Impressive – having stopped smoking. How had he done that? She seemed nonplussed.

He put the key into the lock and turned it, wondering what surprises lurked inside. The opaque glass door opened effortlessly, and he choked on the cigarette as his clean lungs tried to cope with the unfamiliar tobacco.

In the dark, stale air, he reached for the kitchen light switch. The bulb in the centre of the room flashed with the sound of a ting, exposing the pine kitchen table and white fridge on the far side for a brief moment before darkening again.

'The bulb's gone,' she said behind him.

In the grey light of the kitchen window, he dropped the damp mail by the sink.

'Could it be the fuse?' she asked.

Her dark body by the door scared him a little, echoing the detachment he felt from her and everybody else in this future world, but he steadied himself and moved towards the passageway that led to the side door of the house. It was darker in the passageway, and he opened a cupboard door to reach for the fuse box.

Back in the lit kitchen, Janice was smiling and he felt a little better. The kitchen was the same as always with the same cups in the cupboards and the same knives and forks in the drawers. Nothing had changed. Janice began making them a tea with milk that smelt only slightly off, and he decided to go upstairs to change.

At the top of the stairs, he switched on the landing light, glanced at the long mirror on the wall without looking at his face – because he was afraid to see an older person – moved tentatively into his bedroom and turned on the light. The double bed, strutting out from the wall, appeared crumpled on the nearside and reasonably neat on the other: the way he usually left it in the day. The wife's wallpaper was still there, with cream and pale pink flowers on a white background.

Whatever had happened to his wife over these past years? Had they finally arranged a divorce? And what about his daughter, Gemma? Had she visited him at all?

The wind began to howl outside. He twisted the knob of the radiator beneath the window to introduce some heat into the room, opened the doors of his wardrobe and changed into a new shirt, jumper and jeans.

In the en suite bathroom at the far end of the room, he finally looked at himself in the mirror. A middle-aged man with light brown hair, a receding hairline, a thin mouth and a long thin nose with wide nostrils stared back at him. He seemed familiar at first, as if he hadn't aged three and a half years, but with the addition of a small scabby mark in the centre of his forehead that signified the place where he had hit his head at the Zenith site. He would have likely had a similar injury when he crashed his car, hitting his head on the steering wheel.

But as he peered closer at his face, he noticed that something had, after all, changed. The cracks beneath his eyes had grown longer and deeper like Janice's, and his hairline was further receded than it used to be. He felt unnerved. He had never been afraid of middle age or old age, for that matter, but such an increase in years from one day to the next was unsettling. It seemed that even his body was alien to him, as alien as the crazy doctor in the hospital and Janice's head. He'd lost three and a half years and here he was, older with a more wrinkled body.

He closed his eyes and tried to remember something, anything, from the design process. A darkness of impenetrable amnesia appeared before him, and he tried to maintain his composure without succumbing to fear or opening his eyes. What was this amnesia? Where did it come from? The darkness began to give him a dizzying sensation of being sucked into it, similar to the spinning sensation he had felt when crashing his car, so he forcefully and quickly opened his eyes again and walked back into the bedroom.

On the landing, he peered into the study and saw his great oak desk and large drawing board beside it. Both surfaces were covered with papers and plans that were undoubtedly of the building: the only thing he would have been doing for the past three and a half years. Could he really have designed a building that people were praising all over the world as a work of genius? How could he have done such a thing when he'd never designed anything of particular originality, relatively speaking, in the past?

He felt a great urge to go over there and look at the papers, but the fear of not being able to see the plans again, along with the threat of the darkness appearing in his vision, stopped him. He didn't want the same experience that had happened in the Portakabin. He would look at them tomorrow after a good night's sleep. Surely then, he would be able to see them with his memories returning.

He glanced into his daughter's old room. It was still just the way she had left it when she moved out years ago, with pictures of actors on the wall and a map of the world with luminescent highlights of where she wanted to go. The bed was still in the corner. He closed the door and walked back downstairs.

'There's your tea,' Janice said, sitting at the table.

The ghostly sound of the wind buffeted the door as he sat down and opened the damp envelopes he'd collected from the postbox. One was a bank statement, informing him that he had £9018 in his current account. He remembered his wife and wondered whether he was still paying her in monthly instalments. He looked at the statement at the beginning of the month, when his standing order always paid her, and sure enough, on Nov 1, a sum of £800 was paid into the account of Mrs Hillary Gowan. No divorce yet, then. He'd evidently been too busy with the building and too wealthy from the Zenith contract to worry about this ongoing arrangement. The money from his Zenith contract would be in his other account, which he would check later. The other envelope enclosed a card displaying a picture of an idyllic country scene, and inside was written:

'Dad, Hope you're okay. I might contact you soon – it's been a long time. Still in Africa and living well. Congratulations on your building and the beginning of its construction. x'

He held the card tightly with the painful impression that they hadn't seen each other for three and a half years. Why else would she congratulate him on his building now, if she hadn't done so already?

He walked through the sitting room door to check the rest of the house for any signs of change. Upon first glance, the contents of the room were exactly how he had left them three and a half years ago: the Queen Anne leather chairs, the low coffee table in the middle, the objects on the cast-iron fireplace and the plasma television. Beyond the end of the room through the sliding glass doors, a patio and lawn disappeared into the darkening day.

5

In the morning, John loitered at the study doorway, wondering whether to look at the building plans. He had had a bad night, waking up several times and crying out for answers. Now, he desperately wanted to look at them. With his massive amnesia, however, and his inability to see them, blocked by the terrifying, swirling nothingness that seemed to lure him in, he was afraid that there was more to his dizziness yesterday than just the stressful effects of normal concussion, so he decided to look at the plans at work where there were people and the feeling of safety.

On the gravel driveway, his Jaguar had been parked as promised by Pete who had offered to drive it here last night and then get a taxi home. John had apparently parked it in the car park on the night he went to the site and fell.

It was an odd experience to see it again. Its green paint, curvaceous lines and big fat tyres appeared new, as if there had been no past, no crash. What had happened in the minutes after he crashed? Had he woken from unconsciousness and phoned for an ambulance? Had the car been too much of a wreck to drive home?

The press was waiting for him outside his gates.

'Do you remember what happened?' one female reporter

asked, holding a mobile phone at him.

He ignored them and sped away. Driving again through the bend where he crashed was an odd experience, and he tried wrestling with his fears and present predicament in the only way he knew how: by summing up his life. He was forty-eight years old. He was an architect. He had built his house in the leafy countryside between the towns of Blanworth and Toxon ...

Except, he wasn't forty-eight years old: he was fifty-one years old. He wasn't just an architect: he was a world-famous architect. His house wasn't really his house: it was the house of the person who'd been living there for the past three and a half years. Or at least, that's how it felt.

On Blanworth Road, the brown and green fields continued for miles, undulating softly. But as the ground became hilly towards Toxon, concrete cooling towers appeared on the horizon, bellowing plumes of smoke. On the penultimate hill before reaching the valley, the first buildings appeared – something he wasn't used to. He knew this road well and had seen vast changes to the outskirts of Toxon over the past couple of decades, with its boundaries eating into the countryside beyond the valley for car showrooms and fast food joints, but never before had he seen buildings this far out.

The rusty, old town appeared over the last hill. And as he descended into its depths and parked in the multi-storey, he remembered the last time he could recall he had made this journey, on the day he'd learnt about the destruction of the old Zenith building. Where the hell did the last three and a half years go?

He bought a chocolate bun and newspaper in the shopping centre and walked through the centre of town. Nothing seemed very different: the same shops, fashions and teenagers, loitering outside the medieval church before school. When he approached his building, it appeared the same – grey and windowed. On the seventh floor would be his employees, but how would he respond to them? Had they aged like Janice? Were there any new people?

In the foyer, a male receptionist, who he didn't recognise, nodded at him, and John's heart beat faster as he quickly entered the lift. Would people suspect his massive amnesia? Would they find out? The lift opened with a ting, and he walked tentatively down the corridor, wondering how to enter the office – with a confident grin? They would all know he was just out of hospital, so he could simply smile weakly at them, without conversing. All he wanted to do was get inside his private office and look at the building plans.

He opened the door. Four or five people were sitting at their desks behind drawing boards and computers, and a couple were chatting by the water machine, close to Pete's office door on the right of the room. He recognised most of them. He strode forwards down the aisle to his office at the end and was glad everything still looked the same. Employees looked at him with surprise, presumably because he was out of hospital only yesterday. Janice was sitting at her desk outside of his office, like always. She looked up at him with a nonplussed expression and sighed. Today she wore a pink and white striped blouse.

'You're not even supposed to be working today,' she said.

John felt the pleasant sensation that he'd already gained a sense of recent history with somebody since waking in hospital, integrating him a little with this future world: 'Any messages?'

'They're all edited in your inbox. Pete wanted to see you if you turned up. He's got a message from that detective and one from Mann, too.'

Mann was one of the names he didn't recognise on his phone.

He unlocked the door with the same old key and stepped inside. Everything seemed relatively similar: the old beech desk; the black laptop; the leather swivel chair on the other side of the desk; the drawing board, almost two metres in height, by the side of the desk; and the pictures of famous buildings on the walls. What *had* changed was the addition of a grey metal chest of drawers at the back wall and which looked wide enough for A0 sheets of paper.

Around the desk, he glanced nervously at the drawing board. On it was a paper with a drawing plan. But before looking at it properly, he looked away – both excited and afraid of what might happen. The plan had to be of the building: the only thing he would have been working on for the past three and a half years. Would he see it properly now and remember everything?

With a rushing heart, he tried composing himself and

gazed at his old laptop. The lettered keys were a little more faded, and the screen had a couple of new scratches. He opened a desk drawer and found a black notebook. He felt an immediate rush of warmth, like seeing an old friend. It was the one he had used to write the rough measurements at the site before driving home and crashing his car. But like his laptop, like Janice, for that matter, and, indeed, like his own body, it was older now; it was also tatty with white abrasions on the side. He skimmed through it from the back to the front and noticed it was full of writing and diagrams. Near the front, he recognised the words he'd written on what seemed three nights ago but which was really three and a half years ago:

> 'My perimeter walk:
> Length: 60 metres
> Width: 55 metres'

He smiled at the familiar memory whilst wondering how the hell he could have forgotten everything since then. Hurriedly, he put the notebook in his jacket pocket. Ready now to look at the drawing plan, there was a knock at the door immediately followed by Pete walking in, without warning.

'Glad you're up and about,' he said. He pulled a chair from the side of the room and sat opposite John in front of the desk, swiping his hand through his hair that drooped fashionably over his glasses.

John composed himself once more with the knowledge

he would look at the plan soon: 'Thanks for dropping the car off. I drove in this morning.'

'I knocked once on your door but assumed you were asleep, so I got a cab straight back. So you're feeling better now?'

'Not good enough to work properly, but I'm feeling pretty relaxed.'

Pete smiled and swiped his black hair again from his eyes. He looked like a stereotypical architect, always did, wearing black, angular glasses that strangely paralleled his small chiselled face. Today, he was wearing a colourful suit that resembled a Hawaiian shirt. He put a newspaper on the desk in front of John. There was an article marked in pen: 'Have you read this?'

John read:

'The sentencing of Abdulla Hussain has reawakened calls by The Muslim Assembly of Britain for the resignation of Mr Wilkinson Junior employed by his father the CEO of Zenith Star Holdings plc.

Two months after the terrorist attack when the government took the unprecedented step of bailing out Zenith Star which was not insured for terrorism, The Muslim Assembly of Britain, whilst condemning the atrocity, demanded Mr Wilkinson Junior's resignation. They argued that their taxes should not be used to rescue a firm that supplied clothing to the Israeli Army, especially when the CEO's son had made disparaging remarks against Muslims wanting to retrieve land from the Israelis which had incited the attack.

The then Home Secretary, Patti White, said: "Mr Wilkinson Junior's resignation as a condition for saving Zenith Star would be sending the wrong message to terrorists, but any decision lay with Zenith Star alone."

Now that the terrorists have been brought to justice, however, The Muslim Assembly are once again urging the government to put pressure on Mr Wilkinson to demand the resignation of his son. Nobody from Zenith Star was available for comment.'

John looked up: 'So?'

'There's speculation in the tabloids that you were hit on the head by a disgruntled Muslim.'

'I'm sure I wasn't,' John said.

'How so, if you don't remember?'

John was sure nobody hit him because of the almost mystical nature of his amnesia: he knew he was going to be the next architect in the moments before he crashed his car, and he awoke years later as the architect on the very day construction began. It was all too much of a coincidence to be something arbitrary.

'I don't remember what happened to me in the last moments, but the doctor thinks this mark to the head was caused by a fall, and not from me being hit. Even if somebody did push me so that I hit my head on the ground, I don't remember seeing anybody on the site with me.'

'The press need to hear you say that. I just got off the phone with a Detective Murphy who apparently talked to you yesterday, outside the hospital. He's tried to get in contact with you, but your phone has been off. He's worried things could escalate and that there could be race riots in Blanworth again if you don't talk to the press soon. I told Mann who talked to the detective just now on the phone, and he suggested an interview with a reporter at the Zenith offices.'

Mann again. Now John knew he worked for Zenith. And the 'Zenith offices' had to be temporary accommodation until the new building was constructed.

'Why?'

'Because Zenith have been blamed for not sacking Wilkinson Junior, so they want to be seen to be appeasing the moderate Muslims who, in turn, are tired of being blamed for everything.'

'Okay, so the police and Zenith want me to say that I believe I wasn't hit by a Muslim. Fine, I'll talk to the detective and Mann.'

Pete made a move to get up: 'Oh, Mann also said that he hoped to see you at the Chamber of Commerce tonight, if you were feeling up to it. He also apologises for not seeing you in hospital, but he knew you weren't seriously hurt, and he hoped you'd understand, what with how busy Zenith are at the moment.'

John didn't even know what Mann looked like, so he wouldn't dare meet him in his present state, but it didn't matter for now. He hoped his memories would be triggered once he looked at the plans beside him.

Pete's mobile phone rang, and he took his phone out of his pocket: 'Hello… Yep… Okay, I'll be there soon.' He put the phone back in his pocket: 'That was Andrew. He needs me at the site. Do you want to come?'

John remembered the bearded man with Pete in the Portakabin yesterday whom he'd ascertained was the Site Engineer: 'I'm not feeling quite up to it yet. I'll stay here to phone the detective and Mann.'

When Pete left, John readied himself to look at the plans. He took a couple of deep breaths, put on his glasses and swivelled his chair towards them. Vertical, horizontal and diagonal lines appeared on the white paper, and he immediately felt happy and relieved. Unlike yesterday, when he was simply too stressed and not fully recovered from unconsciousness and concussion, he would see the design properly now.

He looked at the lines for a second but couldn't quite appreciate them as a whole, so he retracted his head slightly to get an overall understanding. The lines were joined together in a big network, and he tried staring at it for a moment, but the meaning of the whole alluded him. It was quickly becoming apparent that the drawing was comprised of a random mishmash of straight lines and squiggles. He tried looking at the words beside the lines, all written in pencil.

Again, like the lines, he could ascertain what they were, but to actually understand the meaning of them – what they actually said – was impossible. The letters in the words didn't add up and neither did the lines in the letters. They were unintelligible like a foreign language.

He wasn't afraid at first because he thought he was merely not concentrating enough, so he briefly looked away to gain composure. But when he looked back to the plans and tried reading the words again, the words and drawing began to move and clump together in a swirling, clockwise motion.

Now he *was* scared. Desperation surged through his veins as he remembered the experience yesterday in the Portakabin, but his fear was matched with an abhorrent curiosity, like the lure of watching a real-life execution on YouTube. What the hell was this? A pinprick of darkness appeared at the centre of the swirling mass and quickly grew in size. The page rapidly became a powerful whirlpool of darkness that filled his vision with infinite scope. Images of the spinning road, the bend and the crashing into the ditch flashed before him like lightening as if he had just lived those moments again.

Had he been dreaming everything since apparently waking in hospital? Was he really the architect of the new Zenith building, praised as a work of genius, or was he still in his car, head against the steering wheel, in need of medical assistance and imagining everything? Was the terrifying darkness simply his blackout?

'NOOOOOOOO!' he shouted and grabbed hold of what seemed to be the steering wheel.

The darkness disappeared, and he found himself clutching hold of the plans as he lay on the floor, staring up at the ceiling.

6

In the fading light of his kitchen, John sat for hours, rigid, scared. The kettle, the sink and the outline of the window seemed to change form, as if their three-dimensional quality had become infused with time itself. Difficult questions arose and hovered above the work surfaces. He stared at them with stunned fear, unable to escape. Where had he been these past three and a half years? What was stopping him from seeing the Zenith building? Was his experience since waking in hospital utterly real? Did he really have the talent to be the architect of a building praised as a work of genius across the world?

He approached the dark blue light of the window. The sun was well below the horizon, and dark trees on the edge of the estate waved hauntingly at him. A memory of walking around the destruction of the old building the night he crashed his car floated into view. He remembered taking the measurements and writing them in the first pages of his new notebook: the same tatty book he found earlier in the office, full of words and diagrams.

He retrieved the notebook from his pocket. With the light of his match, he opened the page where he wrote his rough measurements of the building site on the night of the accident:

'My perimeter walk:
Length: 60 metres
Width: 55 metres'

The following page was dated a few days after his car crash: 'Third and fourth floor windows need to be larger to fulfil overall vision, requiring structural adjustments to the…'

He began to feel an incomprehension of what he was reading with the same dizziness he had experienced earlier in the office. He quickly dropped the notebook into the sink, shook the match dead and turned slowly back to the kitchen table. The room was now black, just like everything in his memory from the past three and a half years. Did that time exist? Did he really live those three and a half years? Was he alive or almost dead now, dreaming it all while slumped over his steering wheel with a fatal injury?

With a desperate need to escape the moment, he remembered Pete had mentioned the Chamber of Commerce meeting tonight. Mann, the Vice President of Zenith, would be there. He had apparently joined the company after the destruction of the last building. John knew him exclusively from the amnesiac period. What might happen if he met him? Recollection? If nothing happened, if no memory was triggered and his problems weren't overcome, he would brave his fear of what may be the truth and reveal all to the doctor.

John stood nervously on the High Street opposite Blanworth Town Hall as heavy rain hit his raincoat hood with numerous dull thuds. Four huge Corinthian columns adorned the entrance and above the portico was a decorative triangular pediment with men riding chariots. To the right of the portico was a large room with tall Georgian windows where dark figures lurked, one of whom had to be Mann.

He was fearful of greeting Mann at this Chamber of Commerce meeting and of what he may or may not remember once he saw him, but he couldn't live in fear and do nothing in this world. He had to take positive action. He crossed the street and handed over his raincoat at the reception. In the Central Staircase Hall, he walked up black and white marble steps to a balcony which surrounded the hall on three sides. He approached the front of the building where he stopped at a large oak door on the left that had 'Reception Room' written above it. Muffled talking and laughter emanated from inside. With a rapid heartbeat, he turned the brass handle and pushed.

The room was grand, just the way he remembered it, with 1920s Art Deco bronze and crystal light fittings. Voices echoed softly in the expanse of the high-vaulted ceiling. Groups of people stood with drinks in their hands. The place smelt of damp clothes. He strode as naturally as he could towards the glasses of wine and bowls of crisps in the centre of the room and gulped down half a glass of red. A couple of faces were recognisable: one being the owner of a large delicatessen in Blanworth and another from the council. He would have dealt with the council extensively the past couple of years, during the planning process.

He retreated towards a tall window that looked out onto the High Street and the shopping centre opposite from where he had come. Through the rain and above the electric doors of the shopping centre – one set of many doors around the large complex – was written 'Princegate' in luminescent letters.

Thirty years ago, before the shopping centre was built, a street with old shops and houses had led proudly up to the Town Hall entrance. The council had deemed the destruction of that old street – and others – a necessary sacrifice for the shopping centre.

'Gowan?' a powerful, high-pitched voice asked, behind him.

John was startled and immediately turned to a man he did not recognise. He was broad, though not fat, tall and had a large handlebar moustache which stretched alongside his smile. His brown eyes remained steady and still.

'Hello!' John said, as confidently as possible.

'Glad to see you're up and about.'

Was this Mann? Pete said Mann had hoped to meet him here this evening, and this person was happy to see John. Mann was also called 'Captain', apparently, and this person had a militaristic aura, even a parody of it, with a confident attitude, a large moustache and a striped tie with some military-looking insignia.

'You're okay, then?' the man said.

'Not bad, thanks. I'm feeling a bit better now.'

'Sorry I couldn't contact you directly in hospital, but I've been very busy, what with the first day of construction and the press attention we've been getting, now that the terrorists have been found guilty. Pete told me you were okay which was good enough for me.'

John stared into his big brown eyes and ascertained this had to be Mann because, in addition to the military persona, he obviously worked for Zenith with his direct references to the building.

'Actually, I tried calling your mobile but couldn't get through,' Mann said.

John continued to stare into his eyes, now trying to remember him: 'My phone had run out of battery for a while.'

He looked at the mark on John's forehead: 'A bad knock.'

'The headache's gone.'

'You tripped, then?'

John nodded and rubbed his forehead.

'You remember falling?' Mann asked.

'Not exactly, but I talked to the detective when I left hospital, so I understand the seriousness of the situation. I don't want to be the cause of more race riots in Blanworth if I can possibly help it.'

'Neither do we, which is why I want an interview tomorrow night with you and a reporter at the Zenith offices, to subdue any suspicions.'

'What do you, at Zenith, gain from setting up the interview?'

'We have been blamed for not sacking Wilkinson Junior,

so we want to be seen to be appeasing the moderate Muslims who, in turn, are tired of being blamed for everything. This will relieve a little political pressure we have at the moment.'

'Okay, so you and the police want me to say that I remember tripping – which is fine.'

'Don't lie, necessarily. Just say you are sure that you weren't being followed. I mean, you remember walking onto the site, don't you?'

John nodded.

Mann beamed suddenly and slapped John on the arm: 'You're doing us a great favour. The reporter may ask a couple of questions about the building, too – extra publicity!'

John suddenly felt worried about having to answer questions he knew nothing about if his memory hadn't returned by then: 'What kind of questions?'

'Oh, you know, just how things have been for you in the past few months, and how the building's design, such as the ygje 34 hjed interacts with the ytyy78 ^guibhyde uj in such a way that the tiyuuh yugh…'

John was entranced by Mann's words, so much so that they were beginning to have a dizzying effect; and as he stared at Mann's lips, the sounds exiting them were becoming louder, more blurred and mesmerising. John's balance began to feel lopsided: first one way, then another; and a blackness began to infiltrate his vision.

'Are you okay, Gowan?' Mann asked suddenly.

John realised his arms were stretched outwards in an attempt to regain balance. He tried breathing deeply to instil a sense of composure and felt a sickness at the base of his throat. Mann was staring at him with concern, and John realised he had just entered the beginnings of the world he encountered when staring at the designs of the building; only this time, the information about the building was in audio form as he tried to listen to Mann talk.

'I'm fine, really,' John said, placing both hands on his waist and standing as straight as possible, 'although I'm still feeling the effects of concussion. I will be able to answer questions about my fall. But if the interview goes on for a while and the reporter starts asking questions about the building, perhaps it might be best if Pete comes with me so that he can answer them.'

'Of course, Gowan, especially if you can't remember things.'

John recovered his senses but suddenly felt fearful: 'What do you mean, "can't remember things?"'

'Mann shrugged: 'Oh, nothing, just something that Pete said.'

'What did Pete say?'

Mann paused a moment: 'Well, it's what you didn't say in conversation with him, rather than what you said, that made him think you can't remember things.'

John stared fearfully at him and, as he did so, Mann's moustache seemed to become strangely contorted, as if it were trying to lean back into the skin and hide from the light. Mann's eyes, too, seemed strange. The pupils, steady and solid yet bigger than they should be, staring deeply into

John's soul.

Elsewhere in the room, the 1920s Art Deco bronze and crystal light fittings changed form somehow, no longer pleasant on the eye but coarse and puke-coloured. The high-vaulted ceiling seemed lower, too, as if, with every moment, it was descending upon John's head in a spiral fashion. Objects and people also began to spiral as Mann continued to stare at him. All lines and colours joined together and moved in a clockwise direction and, at the heart of this spiral, a small black dot appeared, quickly growing bigger and bigger, just in the same way as when John had stared at the building plans.

He tried to gain control and an understanding of what was happening to him. Mann suspected his amnesia to at least some limited degree so, with this suspicion, John's world was losing form and solid foundation. It was closing in on him, threatening to consume and annihilate him. It suspected he wasn't the architect of the Zenith building and didn't deserve to be here.

'Noooo!' he shouted, as the room circled around him. 'I remember everything, even the moment I was hit on the head.'

The black hole continued to increase in size and strength, threatening to block everything from view and suck him in.

'Are you okay, Gowan?' Mann asked, disappearing behind the engulfing darkness.

John desperately tried to remain calm: 'I'm just saying, I don't understand what Pete was talking about. I remember everything perfectly.'

'Well, then, you shouldn't have any problem with this interview.'

All of a sudden, the darkness withdrew into a small black dot and vanished. Mann reappeared and the room stopped moving. Mann was staring at him with concern and opened his mouth to say something more, but an elderly, dignified stranger greeted him, and Mann excused himself from John.

John remained standing there, shell-shocked for a couple of minutes and desperately trying to understand what had happened to him. The world had begun to disintegrate and lose form when John was close to revealing his amnesia, and a darkness appeared amidst this confusion, threatening to consume him. Where would it have transported him if he hadn't assured Mann that his memory was fine?

His problems now seemed very real. Far from living in a normal, solid, grounded world, free from any immediate fear of death, he was living in a precarious reality: one which could transport him away to a place of darkness and perhaps death at any moment if it believed John didn't deserve to be here. He couldn't afford to expose himself, no matter what the truth was – or could be.

The doctor was no longer an option. He was a part of this world and, therefore, couldn't be trusted. Could psychology explain John's perfect amnesia, or his inability to see or hear anything about the building, or his original, pure certainty of becoming the Zenith architect before he crashed his car, to wake three and a half years later as the architect of a work of genius?

For the next few minutes, John ambled around the perimeter of the room, exchanging glances with some people he half recognised. No memories were triggered, and staying here now would only risk him talking to somebody else he was supposed to know from the amnesiac period. He drifted to the great wooden door, opened it ajar with his foot and slipped out.

Outside in the rain, with his raincoat back on, he walked up the High Street towards City Square: the same path he had taken when he left the taxi and saw the destruction of the building for the first time in what seemed only several days ago. The thick rain felt good, hiding him safely away from people and things.

The perimeter of the construction site jutted out into the High Street and Square by a few metres. Light from street lamps sparsely illuminated vehicles and cranes. He remembered the random horizontal and vertical lines of the plan, which he saw in the office before he lost consciousness, trying to comprehend them again in his memory; but he couldn't unify them into a comprehensive whole, and a blankness began to overcome him as before; so he stopped thinking about it, fearing he might faint.

A shabby-looking man appeared on the bench in the middle of the Square; he was very still and almost camouflaged by the grey rain. As John approached him, the sound of rain hitting his tatty leather jacket became louder than the heavy rain on the ground, like incessant gunfire. Water dripped from his beard into his lap.

'You found me lying on the site the other night, didn't you?' John said loudly.

The tramp remained still, rooted to the iron lattice bench and the solid brick ground. He seemed like a part of City Square: born from the surroundings with his greys merging into the rain. The police had often moved him on, but they had never been successful in permanently moving him away.

'I wanted to thank you.'

The man still didn't move. John knew he wasn't deaf, because he remembered Janice saying that the tramp had used John's mobile to call the ambulance; John also remembered talking to him on the night he crashed his car, although that was years ago now. He suddenly feared the man was dead, because he was so still. John stepped back but, as he did so, the tramp's head shuddered, and John cried out with shock before controlling himself.

'I thought you were dead,' John said.

The tramp's head swayed from left to right but did not look up at John: 'You, too?'

'Who else thinks you're dead?'

'Me, sometimes.'

The rain died a little, and John felt that he didn't need to talk so loudly: 'Do you remember me?'

'Aye,' he said, not looking up.

John wasn't convinced: 'I wanted to thank you for what you did in calling the ambulance the other night.'

The tramp grunted. The sound was primordial, as if

emanating from centuries past, deep beneath the concrete ground.

'Do you remember three and a half-years ago when I stumbled around the wreckage of the old building at night?'

The tramp remained still, patient, as if waiting for something – perhaps death. A drop of silver snot appeared at the end of his nose.

'But why would you?' John said despondently, lowering his voice: 'It was a long time ago.'

'I remember you, Mr Gowan.'

John was surprised and waited a moment for him to embellish. He seemed to hold an answer to something hidden and close by: an answer that had been unattainable to John since waking in hospital.

'You see, I'm looking for something,' John said impatiently.

The tramp slowly moved his head upwards. His face was mottled with scabs. One fake eye stared into the sky, but his real eye focussed intently on John: 'What would that be?'

John tried to remember the design process and closed his eyes, but the oppressive darkness of the amnesia stared back at him, so he opened them again: 'A time behind the darkness.'

'Aye,' the tramp said, in a matter of fact tone.

The tramp seemed to dispel the fear that this world wasn't real in these moments, leaving only mystery. There was an odd, personal connection between them. The tramp had been with him on both nights either side of the amnesia: the night John took measurements at the site before going on to crash his car, and the night before construction began when the tramp used John's mobile phone to telephone for an ambulance. The amnesia, guarded by this gatekeeper.

'Do you know what I'm talking about?' John said.

The tramp looked down towards John's shoes as if he'd given up with the conversation.

John began to feel despondent, realised his impression of the tramp was beginning to play tricks on him this dark night and wanted to go.

'I do!' the tramp said with sudden ferocity, his head rising quickly and his teeth suddenly appearing beneath his dry rubber lips – like a piranha's mouth.

Surprised by the outburst, John stumbled back and tripped over his own shoe. The air rushed passed his ears, and he hit the ground hard on his tailbone. He just managed to hold his head up to save it from hitting the concrete, too.

'There you go, falling again,' the tramp said, cackling with laughter.

Shocked and vulnerable, John scrambled to his feet with a wet back and almost fell again. He felt compelled to kick him and demand what he meant, but fear of the tramp seized him as the man continued to laugh, almost as if he knew more than John was prepared to know, so John turned quickly and walked towards the Norman Gate on the north side of the Square. He was not running away, he told himself. The tramp was crazy and not worth talking to.

The yellowy white stone arch, lit by electric light, passed above as the rain briefly stopped and footsteps echoed. The tramp's voice was long gone. On the other side, the grand cathedral appeared. Ablaze with artificial light, it towered into the night with three huge, recessed arches adorning its western front. On top were tall spires that were far bigger than any ordinary church spire, and towards the back was a large square tower with four spires of its own. John did not believe in God, but he did believe in this building, and if there were any place on earth he could feel comfort, it was here.

He walked along a gravel pathway that cut through the large front lawn and approached the main entrance. Above the entrance were stained glass windows and various decorations and embellishments carved into the stone, all of which were dwarfed by, and housed within, the central arch. He passed beneath the arch and stepped up to the great oak door. The round metal handle was cold to the touch and loose, but the door was locked. He turned, sat on the steps and looked fearfully back to the Norman archway from whence he had come. Tonight, the cathedral offered him a little warmth and a place of sanctuary, but the amnesia was still too frightening to allow him adequate escapism.

Rain continued to pour a metre away from his feet, and small puddles peppered the gravelly pathways that criss-crossed the lawn. As a result of his fall, the underside of his trousers were wetter than the rest of his clothes and sticking to his legs; a small bruise on his tailbone made it a little uncomfortable to sit. He had the option of walking back to the car, which he had parked in Princegate shopping centre car park but, to do so, he would have to pass the Square where the tramp would be waiting: a crazy old man who, nevertheless, evoked the frighteningly mysterious aspect of the amnesia. John could go another way, through another archway elsewhere, and eventually end up on the other side of the shopping centre; but first, he would close his eyes for a moment and listen to the rain hitting the gravel – a sound that helped to drown his fears.

He awoke shivering and to the sound of birds singing. Arched shapes of sunlight lit distant parts of the lawn. He couldn't remember dreaming. His body was an obstacle to a couple of people walking towards the oak doorway, which was now open, but they paid no attention to him. His head was at an odd angle, wedged against the stone archway, and his torso and legs felt like a trodden worm – squashed and somewhat detached.

With aching bones and the help of a demonic gargoyle for leverage, he hoisted himself up. He remembered Mann from last night, whose presence hadn't triggered anything from his memory. Mann seemed like a relic from the Empire Days with his broad handlebar moustache and practical way of speaking. That people referred to him as 'Captain' was understandable, because he certainly seemed to have the appearance of somebody who had been in the army. The fact of not remembering such an eccentric character and then experiencing terrifying darkness that had appeared when Mann suspected his amnesia had been shocking, but John couldn't afford to believe he was not living in the real world.

He retrieved his mobile phone from his pocket and called Pete.

'Yep?' a nasal voice said.

'I went to the Chamber of Commerce last night and talked to Mann. I told him that I'd do the newspaper interview.'

'Good.'

John had to be careful not to reveal his amnesia whilst, at the same time, proving to people he could remember everything. It was Pete that had told Mann about John's possible amnesia.

'However, I've felt on and off since coming out of hospital. The doctor told me to take it easy and not work, so it might be best if you were there in case the reporter asks questions about the building, itself, and I don't feel up to it. Mann agrees it would be a good idea, and you've been on the construction site the last couple of days, so you might be in a better position to answer any up-to-date questions, too.'

'Okay, John, that won't be a problem.'

John ended the phone call and closed his eyes again. There had to be a way of validating this existence. There had to be a truth he could find that made everything real and explained why and how he was here. There had to be an explanation for his amnesia that validated his present existence. He walked along the gravel path that separated the grass, through the medieval gate and across the High Street that led seamlessly onto the Square. A lot of noise came from the site where workers were shouting and diggers were crunching, and the tramp was no longer to be seen.

7

At home in his study, John needed to find the address of the temporary Zenith offices where he would be attending tonight. He looked inside his oak desk and found an old letter dated from the amnesiac period. At the top of the letter, it read:

G R Mann
Company Secretary
Zenith Star Holdings Ltd
Floor 9
Regis Building
40 Aylsham Road
Blanworth BL3 9XT

He knew this area in Blanworth not far from the city centre. Happy now that he could find the location, John felt intrigued by the letter, it being written to him from the amnesiac period, and continued reading:

'Dear Mr Gowan and Mr Williams
    Following our letter of [date], advising you of your Partnership's inclusion in the shortlist of tenders for

the design and management of the construction of a building at Blanworth, and our subsequent meetings, I can now inform you that you have been selected as the preferred bidder.

Since time is of the essence, a copy of this letter and a draft contract have been forwarded to your solicitors, Messrs Graham and Surly. Some clauses of the contract need urgent discussion with you. In this regard, perhaps you would kindly telephone this office for a mutually convenient time.

We are delighted to welcome you on board and look forward to a close and profitable relationship. Yours sincerely

G R Mann
Company Secretary'

John didn't encounter any of the dizzying problems he had experienced when looking at the notes in his notebook or the building designs, because the letter didn't reveal design aspects of the building, itself. Ignoring his doctor's advice to rest, he now felt invigorated to learn more information about the amnesiac period, especially as he was going to the Zenith offices tonight with the intention of disguising his amnesia. Perhaps new information might trigger his memory before then.

He opened his laptop and tried accessing his emails. His old password had changed, but the email account offered security questions which he could answer and, finally, he got into his account. There were many emails dated over the past couple of days since waking in hospital. Ignoring these, he looked at older ones. Many were correspondence with Zenith, similar to the letter he had just read, and some revealed design information about the building which John could not read; he looked away quickly before losing a sense of reality.

For the next two hours, he avidly read over information indirectly linked to the building, such as construction company details, financial dealings, dates and times. Grey area information that hinted at the design, such as materials and amounts, proved to be impossible.

On the way to Blanworth, the countryside appeared mysterious in the sun with great tramlines passing through green autumnal fields towards a bare, stark horizon. It frightened him, but there was a beauty to it, too. When the land became absolutely flat and the far-off cathedral appeared – its tall spires visible for miles around – he glanced at the letter on the passenger seat which had the address of the temporary Zenith offices.

On the other side of town, he left the inner ring road and headed back toward the City Centre. A large, semi-circular building, several stories high with maroon-coloured brick and reflective-mirrored windows, concavely faced the side of the road, and in the concave space, behind neatly trimmed bushes and a yellow road barrier, was a car park. Beside the barrier, a sign read: 'REGIS Offices available now. Short term. Long term. Your terms.' He opened his wallet and, to his relief, found a yellow card with the word 'Regis' written along the top. He inserted the card into the machine, and the barrier rose.

With satchel in hand, he looked up at the building – its mirrored glass reflecting a darkening red sky – and counted to floor nine. Zenith was on the top floor. Through the central door, the lighting was dim with one flickering bulb on the wall.

A security man was dressed in a black coat with yellow lines across it: 'Identification, please?'

John hoped his driving licence was good enough.

The man held a machine, typing a couple of buttons, and smiled: 'Thank you, Mr Gowan, you're expected on floor nine.'

As the lift began its ascent, John's throat tightened and became dry. Where would he go, once the doors opened? He couldn't remember this building, yet he would have been here many times before, liaising with Zenith over the design plans. He had wanted to meet Pete in the car park before they went in, just to have somebody to follow to Mann's office, but Pete had sent a text saying he was detained at the site and would be here as soon as possible.

The lift opened sooner than he wanted, and ahead was an open area, followed by a red-carpeted corridor that disappeared into the distance in a gradual bend. He stepped into the open area.

'He's in there, Mr Gowan,' a voice said, to his right.

John turned and saw a well-dressed young man, sitting behind a reception desk. Behind the young man, a darkly tainted window highlighted his blond hair. John wondered whether he'd met him before.

'Do you mean Mann?' John said.

'Yes.'

John was afraid to ask which room for fear of exposing his amnesia, but he had no choice: 'Whereabouts?'

The man lowered his eyebrows slightly: 'Mr Wilkinson's office.'

'Oh, I thought we might be meeting in Mann's office.'

The young man smiled and shook his head with slight movements.

John turned towards the corridor. It appeared long as it curved away. He began walking. The sumptuous red carpet felt buoyant, but the walls were a dreary, greyish white with the odd corkboard displaying messy post-its, and cheap-framed pictures depicting countryside scenes. He felt a little deja vu, as if the lines of separation between him, the carpet, the walls and the things on the walls overflowed into each other; and he wondered whether his memory was trying to poke through into his consciousness.

Half a minute later, he began to wonder how the corridor could be this long inside this building. The building didn't seem that big from the outside. He looked side to side, glancing at the doors – none of which were numbered – and wondered whether he had passed the correct door.

Finally, the corridor ended in the distance with a door

that was different from the rest – varnished oak with a pretty grain. John guessed it could be Wilkinson's room by its distinction from the others.

He approached and touched the door's golden handle which felt cold against his hand. There was a high, but powerful male voice emanating from inside, and he recognised it to be Mann's from yesterday at the Town Hall. Would Wilkinson be there, too? John couldn't remember Wilkinson on a personal level, either: a man he was supposed to have met several times during the design process, according to his correspondence. Wilkinson had, however, been on the News before the design process as a softly spoken American and had, occasionally, appeared at Chamber of Commerce meetings, so John knew what he looked like. John wondered whether it was not too late to turn away, but the golden handle seemed to turn of its own accord, like a Ouija board.

A large, bright room appeared with four Queen Anne chairs to the left-of-centre, facing each other; they were similar to John's sitting room chairs with studded wings and brown leather. Behind them, further to the left, a window displayed a green horizon beyond the city, and a darkening sky slashed with oranges and reds. John closed the door behind him and noticed Mann to the right, standing rigidly beside a large oak desk. Behind Mann, a darkly tinted window displayed shadowy city buildings.

'Gowan's here now,' Mann said into his mobile phone with a big grin that stretched with his moustache like an elastic band. He put the phone in his pocket and moved towards John: 'No Pete?'

'He's delayed at the site but should make it to the interview.'

'It's good he's coming. He can talk about construction at the site in the last couple of days. Good publicity!'

John wondered why Mann called Pete by his first name and himself by his surname; he hoped, having undoubtedly dealt with Mann a lot more than Pete in the design process, it might be a term of endearment, Mann having been in the army. On the desk beside Mann was a family photo of a man surrounded by children. He had silver hair, combed back around his ears, and piercing blue eyes. John recognised him to be Wilkinson, presumably with his grandchildren.

'Will Wilkinson be joining us?' John said.

'Oh, no, but he wished you luck and sends you his regards.'

John was relieved. There was too much to worry about today than to deal with another memory problem.

'Your memory's fine to answer questions about the building if Pete doesn't get here?' Mann asked, as if reading John's mind.

The chairs and the window seemed to change without changing, as if escaping the relativity of comparison, whereby everything else might have changed too, so as not to make it reasonable to assume that they had changed. They might have grown ten times in size or ten times as small, whilst everything else, including John's own body, had done just the same to disguise their change. Soon, everything would begin to spiral, and John would be sucked in towards the black hole that formed at the centre.

Seized by fear, John tried to gain control of the situation: 'Of course, I told you yesterday that my memory is fine. I only want Pete to be here because I'm still suffering a little from the concussion, and I might not necessarily want to answer a lot of questions. The doctor told me to rest.'

Mann grinned and tapped John on the back with a powerful hand.

The room still seemed inexplicably odd, but at least it hadn't begun to spiral.

There was a knock at the door, followed by an opening. A thin man with black hair and slightly hunched shoulders walked in and looked at both John and Mann with a smile. It was Detective Murphy who wore the same navy-blue suit as the other day outside the hospital.

'You found us alright then,' Mann said.

'The blond lad at the desk directed me.'

They all sat down in the armchairs where, between the chairs, there was a coffee table with a jug of water, a teapot, glasses and cups. A small chandelier hung above, and equestrian paintings hung nearby on the wall.

'We have almost an hour before the reporter turns up, so what should Gowan say in this interview?' Mann said to Murphy, whilst they made drinks. 'And is there anything he shouldn't say?'

For the next few minutes, the men discussed the interview, confirming exactly what John should and shouldn't say about the circumstances leading up to his fall, and how he should say it. He needed to sound certain, deliberate and utterly convinced of what had happened to him, even if he couldn't remember the fall, itself.

Half an hour later, Mann received a telephone call from the receptionist who told him the reporter had arrived, and Mann told him to escort the reporter to Wilkinson's room. Only one reporter was allowed by Zenith, and he represented Blanworth Express, the local newspaper.

When he walked in, he wore a grey suit, a brown tie, a white shirt – none of which were pressed – and carried a multi-coloured rucksack. His hair was wavy brown and his skin, ghostly white.

Mann shook his hand: 'Hello, I'm Captain Mann, Vice President of Zenith. We spoke on the phone, I believe?'

'Yes, I'm Palmer for Blanworth Express.'

'Gowan,' John said, shaking his hand.

The reporter looked keenly at him.

'Detective Murphy,' the policeman said. 'Good to finally meet you in person.'

'Likewise,' the reporter said.

As they sat, he put a pocket-sized notebook on his lap and a silver digital recording device, the size of his hand, on the table: 'You don't mind me using this, do you?'

'No, that's not a problem,' Mann said.

He pressed a button on the device and looked at John: 'On the night of the 7th of November, can you tell me why you decided to go to the Zenith site?'

John prepared himself a moment before speaking: 'It was the last night before construction began, and I wanted to go to the site to think about the future. I had nothing to do, as such. I just wanted to prepare mentally for the next day and walk around the site.'

'Were you on your own?'

'Yes.'

'Did you tell anybody you would be there at that time?'

Since waking in hospital, nobody had told John that they knew he was there at that time: 'No. It was a last-minute decision to go.'

'So, where were you when you decided to go to the Zenith site?'

'At home.'

'Where's home?'

John pointed at the recording device: 'I'd rather not broadcast where I live, even though it's easy for people to find out.'

Palmer nodded and glanced down at his notepad: 'That's okay. Just a rough idea would be fine.'

'In the countryside between Blanworth and Toxon.'

'And how did you get to the site?'

'By car.'

'Did you notice anybody following you whilst you drove to Blanworth?'

'No.'

'Once you got to Blanworth, where did you park?'

'In Princegate shopping centre car park. Then I walked through the shopping centre and into City Square. I walked through the Square, passing the tramp on his bench, walked up the side road of the Zenith site and onto the site.'

'And you didn't see anybody following you?'

'No.'

'Did you see anybody there, waiting for you?'

'Nope.'

Palmer paused and remained staring at John, like a ghost with his deathly white complexion: 'Then what happened?'

'I unlocked the gate and walked around the site for a minute. Then I can't remember anymore.'

'So you can't remember how you got that big mark on your forehead?'

'That's correct.'

'And then what do you remember?'

'Waking up in hospital.'

'What did the doctor say about your injury?'

'He told me I had concussion and that he believed I had had a fall. The injury was caused by my head hitting the ground.'

'But how did you fall?'

'I must have tripped over something. There's a lot of rubble about.'

Palmer stared at John a moment, then turned to Murphy: 'On the phone, you said you would check CCTV evidence for anybody following Mr Gowan.'

'Which I have done and, other than the tramp – information I believe I gave you on the phone – nobody followed John. There is no CCTV in the side road so, in theory, somebody could have come from the other direction, but the tramp, who followed John a few seconds after John had passed him in the Square – as shown by CCTV footage in the Square – saw nobody leave the site, and John remembers seeing nobody as he approached the site entrance before he went in.'

'Could someone have been there, waiting for him on the site?'

'As John said, the site itself was locked so, if they were on the site, they would have had to have climbed over the eight-foot-high hoarding. John, however, remembers seeing nobody as he walked onto the site.' He sighed. 'Of course, we can speculate theories, but we, the police, have found no evidence to suggest otherwise.'

Palmer dropped his gaze to the floor, resignedly. Unfortunately for him today, whatever his sensationalist need for John to have been hit by someone – the implication of a Muslim, especially – there would be no such gratification.

'It appears doubtful that anybody hit Mr Gowan then,' he said.

A wave of purity surged through the room, cleansing its contents of any malevolent appearance. The objects seemed clear, distinct and friendly. The Queen Anne chairs appeared comfortable; the equestrian pictures seemed lively and joyful, and the darkening world outside made the inside feel cosy and habitable.

John was very pleased, feeling more united with this future world and closer to his true self as the architect of the Zenith building, safe from the threat of being transported away to a place of darkness. He had come here to satisfy Zenith and the police, and he had done it, fulfilling his responsibilities as architect of the Zenith building. He now had to continue acting and behaving as his true self, concealing his problems and uniting with this future world. Perhaps soon, all his problems would go away, and memories from the amnesiac period would return. It was true that Mann and Pete had their suspicions about John's amnesia, but if he could just continue convincingly into this evening, then maybe tonight or tomorrow his problems would go away: his memories would return and he would become the architect of the Zenith building unto himself. The alternative truth, the parallel world where he did not design the building, would disappear completely.

The reporter poured himself a drink of water: 'Can we talk a little about the building then? How has construction been so far? Is everything on schedule?'

Pete still wasn't here to save John from these questions: 'I'm not sure I can do any more questions – now that the important ones are out of the way. My doctor told me not to work for a few days after the concussion, and I shouldn't really be here.'

'Oh, of course,' the reporter said.

'Everything is going well,' Mann said. 'We're digging the foundations at the moment. We had hoped Pete Williams the partner in John's firm would be here, but he's detained at the site. He's been there since John had his accident.'

The reporter nodded: 'I don't want to ask anything that

might cause Mr Gowan undue stress. It's just that a couple of days ago, in the Blanworth Express, I wrote an article entitled "The Freedom Building". It said…' He looked down at his notes.

'"… The new Zenith building, which has adopted the unofficial moniker "The Freedom Building", is seen by many, including politicians, councillors and members of the press, as the face of freedom, not only because it defiantly rises from the ashes of the previous building which was destroyed by terrorists, but because its design, its sheer innovative quality appears free."

'Did you intend to make it appear free, Mr Gowan?'

John began to feel nauseous and remembered seeing the newspaper article, entitled "The Freedom Building", in his hospital bed, although he didn't read all of it and hadn't read that part: 'I think I'll let people make up their own minds as to whether it appears free.'

'But you must have known that this building would be viewed as a political symbol of freedom, as much as anything else, and, therefore, designed it with that in mind, didn't you?'

The easy answer would be to agree, but then he would have to qualify it with an explanation, based on the building's actual appearance. The sickness rose from his stomach to the base of his neck. Without knowing what to say, he blurted an evasive reply: 'It's a bit of an American idea, isn't it? We're not "Land of the Free".'

Mann looked at John with concern.

John tried to calm himself and integrate with the conversation: 'Although we *are* a free country, and America *is* our closest ally.'

He felt the sickness well in his throat and tried to be more professional so that he did not contradict anything he might have said publicly during the amnesiac period: 'I just don't feel, at the moment, I want to be telling other people how to see the building. If you think it appears free, then great. But others might think it looks like something else.'

'But surely you can tell us the idea you had for designing the building?' Palmer said.

Luminescent blotches began to appear in front of John's eyes in addition to the sickness which was spreading into his mouth. He felt very dizzy and not far from falling from his chair: 'I think I don't feel well enough to be answering questions about the building. I'm terribly sorry.'

The reporter stared at him incredulously for a moment, then turned to Mann: 'In a previous interview with the Blanworth Express, you said you chose Mr Gowan's building because it appeared free so, now that the building has adopted the unofficial moniker "The Freedom Building" , propounded by reporters such as me, you must be pleased?

'Of course.'

'So I'll put the question to you: did you choose Mr Gowan's design for political reasons?'

Mann lowered his bushy eyebrows: 'Could you explain what you mean by "political"?'

'Well, the previous building was destroyed by terrorists

who reacted to Wilkinson Junior's derogatory comments about Muslims, as he put it, wanting to reclaim land from the Israelis. A new building that artistically expresses the notion of freedom would seem to suggest, at the very least, the freedom to express opinion without fear of retribution.'

'Would you give me just a moment, please?' Mann said as he got up, walked to the other side of the room behind Wilkinson's great desk and called somebody on his mobile phone.

Palmer glanced at John with a look of bemusement, then span a pencil expertly around his fingers. John began to feel better as the attention was no longer on him, although the room and the reporter did appear somewhat strange. Indecipherable murmurings came from Mann on the other side of the room, shortly followed by his return.

'I'm sorry about that. I hope you won't put this little interlude in your article. It would make us look unprofessional!' Mann grinned.

'Not if you have something to say,' Palmer said, smiling back.

Mann paused and thought carefully: 'Firstly, Wilkinson Junior's comments that provoked the terrorist attack were a mistake and did not reflect the ethos of Zenith. He has apologised profusely on several occasions and is profoundly sorry. Secondly, we, nevertheless, believe in the freedom to express opinion without fear of retribution. Thirdly, we believe in freedom in terms of democracy, the rule of law and capitalism – all of which are important to a business like ours. So, in answer to your question, we did choose Mr Gowan's design for political reasons, because we saw all these qualities reflected in its artistic freedom.'

Palmer smiled, nodded and turned to John: 'So, if you're feeling a little better, could you tell me what you were thinking when you managed to conceive the kljh kjjh 87y…'

John watched Palmer's mouth move and tried to listen, but immediately realised he could not understand what he was saying. He had to be talking about the design, itself. He stopped trying to listen and waited for the reporter's mouth to stop moving.

The room, nevertheless, continued to feel strange: slanted, perhaps, as if the floor had risen one end and the walls tilted in odd directions. The effect was not static but mobile, like being on board a ship. Words exiting the reporter's mouth travelled sideways through space and seeped into different objects, reverberating them accordingly: a 'shhh' from the ornate picture frame, a 'grrr' from the coffee table and a 'ckkkllleee' from the chandelier above.

John felt a dark, insidious force from the room, dizzying his head and inviting him to forget the reason it was happening. He knew it was beginning to suck him in, despite no darkness yet visibly appearing, and he battled to keep himself in control. The tilted walls began to collapse inwards, pressing upon the space of the sitting men. He felt imprisoned but, within the maelstrom of blurred words, one word was understandable and brought a kind of scorching fire to the air: 'freedom.'

The room became worse, more active, and he and the men seemed to begin moving around the coffee table. John held tightly onto the chair, hoping that what he was feeling couldn't possibly be real, but his senses were, nevertheless, utterly convinced that he was moving towards a great force – a dark truth underlying the fabric of this room. Battling hard to remain in control, he tried to appear normal to the others, as if nothing was happening, but he didn't know how much longer he could continue. Perhaps it would be best if he fell onto the floor to show he hadn't yet fully recovered, but then what would happen to him? Would Mann see that answering questions about the building was an impossibility for him? Would he disappear from this world forever?

A blurry figure walked into the room. John felt the sensation of being on a ride at an amusement park whilst trying to spot a friend in the crowd, but the person was wearing something like a colourful suit, and he realised it must be Pete. Pete's presence would not help, though, because the questions the reporter was asking were reserved specifically for the architect. It was John who had designed the building and, therefore, only he could explain why he had designed it in a particular way. Pete sat down in the empty chair and greeted the others. His low, nasal voice pierced the spinning room.

John wondered how he could possibly continue in this world, even if he survived this interview. How could he pretend to be the designer of the building over the next few days, weeks and months? Indeed, did he want to? Maybe the alternative, whatever it might be, was better? As he asked himself the question, a terrifying darkness began to appear in the centre of the coffee table. The table wasn't simply black as a result of fading light. The darkness was an entity in itself, a revealed truth, as if the reason underlying the reality of everything in the room, the world and John's existence had opened up. Its elemental force was vigorously pulling him towards it as the room's lines and colours began to encircle it.

'Are you okay, Gowan?' Mann's high-pitched, resonant voice asked – somewhere.

John desperately tried to nod.

'You seem confused,' Mann said. 'You really don't have to answer the question. You've already told him you don't want to. It's obvious you don't look well.'

' *I* can answer some of the questions now. That's why I'm here,' Pete's low-pitched, nasal voice said, consolingly.

'But you didn't design the building, Mr Williams,' the reporter said, 'so you couldn't answer this particular question.'

Both Pete and Mann suspected that John had amnesia, although to what extent John didn't know. Soon too, so might everybody else. To allow Pete to take over would only heighten the men's suspicions that John couldn't remember anything about the building. John knew this, but what could he do? The problem in this present moment had been anticipated, and John had simply been prepared to let Pete answer questions, but this didn't mean John's life would get any easier. Indeed, to ignore the question now might be the end for John. The black hole was growing. This world might not accept John's explanation that he was suffering from concussion and, therefore, couldn't answer the question. The black hole epitomised his amnesia, and it may now be too powerful to overcome.

In the terror of the moment, an idea suddenly occurred to him: one that would incentivise Pete, at the very least, to dismiss any concerns about John's amnesia and, consequently, convince Mann that nothing was wrong with John's memory. It was an idea reliant on Pete's extraordinary ego. It was an horrific idea, and John's problems would certainly not be overcome completely as a result, but it might at least offer an intermediate solution.

As the idea settled in his head, so the room settled down to stillness, and the darkness seeped back into the coffee table, disappearing from view, as if it could no longer smell John's fear of not being able to connect with this world. His blood seemed to rush to one side of his body as if his momentum continued, but the walls retreated a little, appearing less malevolent and threatening. This was the proof he needed. All the men were looking at him with concern.

'I'm sorry,' Palmer said and appeared genuinely apologetic. 'I'll ask another question – one for Mr Williams about construction so far.'

'No, I'd like to say something,' John said, recovering his equilibrium. 'I am feeling a little unwell, as you know, but, aside from that, I think Pete would be able to answer the question, because conscience cannot allow me to take the full glory of designing the building anymore.'

Pete lowered his manicured eyebrows beneath the rim of his glasses and down as far as they would go, leaving a trail of forehead ripples in their wake.

'The press have described me, thus far, as being the designer whilst my employees and partner in the firm, Pete Williams, helped complete the details of my vision, but I think everybody should know that Pete had an equal share in the creative process of designing the building.'

John stood, full of nervous energy, and began clapping: 'Pete Williams, you deserve the credit, too, as joint designer of the building.'

Pete's eyes widened. Mann and the reporter were still for a moment. John turned to them, clapping, and they began to clap, too. A broad grin erupted on Pete's face as everybody clapped. John felt the stress of the past minute exit his body through his skin.

'Now that that's official,' John said, glancing at the reporter, 'I'll let Pete answer the previous question about the building.'

'Well,' Pete said, looking at the reporter, 'I'll try.' He sat on the edge of the chair, clearly overwhelmed by the moment and very happy. 'May I first have a sip of water?'

'Of course,' Mann said. He seemed pleased with John's outburst, smiling broadly with his large moustache.

The reporter seemed thoroughly satisfied with this interview, too, happy that he was the one to report this announcement. He repeated the question to Pete.

Pete leaned towards the table, picked up the jug of water, poured some water into a glass and sipped. He sat back into the chair, paused a moment and began: 'Well, the *76h ijhb IUh…'

John stopped listening but kept looking at Pete, knowing how well he would answer the reporter in a creative way – all as the lie that he jointly designed the building. Pete was always a good talker and marketeer: important aspects of being a modern architect, and the main reasons John invited him as a partner in the beginning.

The relinquishing of John's status as sole designer of the building offered an escape from the darkness. It was a painful solution – one which sickened his heart – because his true, artistic self would never now be fully acknowledged by the world, but what other choice did he have in these moments? It would enable John to be left alone by the media and even by Zenith, because Pete could permanently take over until John's problems were overcome. John could now concentrate on tackling his amnesia and all other problems related to the building.

The rest of the interview went smoothly, and John left them an hour later to go home. The reporter apparently went back to work, fully satisfied with John's and Pete's answers. Murphy was happy too, and had thanked John, Pete and Mann for their help in evading further tensions in Blanworth

8

At home, after resting a couple of days, John tried redesigning the Zenith building. It would be reasonable to assume that he could begin from where he had lost his memory on the night he crashed his car and commence designing it just as he would have done then. On that night in the moments before he crashed, he had been certain he would design a work of genius that Zenith would have to accept; but now, he couldn't capture the same ineffable inspiration, and there seemed to be nothing he could do to create a work of genius. The little he was able to know about the building's design was that it appeared free, but what did freedom look like?

Over the next few months, John's condition didn't change, so he allowed Pete to continue working at the site and also permitted him to be interviewed by radio stations and newspapers about the building, which Pete thoroughly enjoyed, utilising his social talent. John was still glad he had announced him as joint architect, because it kept public attention away from himself and indicated to the world that John was not comfortable with fame – so much so that he was now reported as working on other things. Pete had so much of an ego and wanted so badly to be seen as the Zenith architect that it seemed he was willing to believe the lie, himself.

But John's failure to redesign the building and connect with its architect was giving him a growing sense of unreality in the world – in a way he couldn't quite describe. There was no imminent threat of darkness, not unless he looked directly at the plans of the building or its actual construction, but the unreality made him feel he had little in common with anything or anybody. In fact, it was reminiscent of the way he had always felt, to a lesser degree, throughout his adult life, never connecting fully with the outside world.

He awoke with his head on the ground. Spitting mud, he pushed himself to a seated position. Woodland birds twittered. His head pounded with pain, and he felt very thirsty. A large oak loomed ahead. The thought of simply leaning against it and closing his eyes gave him some hope of peace.

Where was he? Last night at home, he had despaired of the continual problems since waking in hospital six months ago. With a bottle of whisky, he had left his garden in the darkness and continued into the woods.

Now in daylight, he walked a little way until entering a large farmer's field with light green grass. He had expected to see the back of his house but was obviously on the wrong side of the wood, so he turned to walk back but stumbled and fell backwards into the field. A blue sky with wispy trails of cloud dazzled him – a rare hot day for spring.

The people of Blanworth and Toxon were making the most of this hot weekend: beer men, fat women, tarty women, blankets in back gardens, sunglasses covering closed eyes, unread books beside lifeless lives, paddling pools, kids with water pistols, and oily-faced men doing up cars – but knowing nothing about cars – with radios blaring. There were boy racer cars, air-conditioned golf clubs, hard-working farmers, teenagers in bed, prisoners playing football, cancer sufferers watching the final stages of a golf tournament on television from the final stages of life, bird mating calls, benefits' tenants collecting food stamps, and one motorbike fatality with leather burned into the skin. John remembered how he had wanted to move away from Blanworth into the countryside to get away from people and things.

Under tree cover again, he stumbled through bracken, for what seemed several minutes, until he recognised his overgrown lawn and derelict, mucky pond – guarded by the wife's tasteless gnomes – appearing through the trees. He grabbed hold of the last oak tree, its rough bark grazing his hand, and looked beyond the garden to the back of his house.

Twenty years ago, the previous house was occupied by an elderly couple. Apparently, one of them had left a lit cigarette in the thatched loft. They were saved from the blaze, but the house was completely destroyed, and they went on to a nursing home. John had had the opportunity to design something original, but the wife had wanted a traditional house with slate roof, dormer windows, grey brick and a patio at the back.

Desperate for orange juice, John mounted the hard stone patio on all fours like a crocodile, reached for the sliding doors and fell into the sitting room. The blue, buoyant carpet felt soft on his face, and he remembered how he had believed he was happy when his wife was living with him here. He had designed a house in the countryside – albeit, an unoriginal one – he had his own architectural company, which was reasonably successful locally, and he had a loving family. How couldn't he have been happy?

He hobbled through the door into the stark kitchen with his back bent and drank orange juice straight from the carton. Its coldness compounded his headache, and he dropped the carton which spilled over the pine table. He remembered a note that had once been there:

'We're going, John. I hope you can understand, Hillary and Gemma.'

Life obviously hadn't been happy for them. Hillary had blamed him for not expressing emotion to either her or their daughter – whatever that meant. She'd fed lies to their daughter about him which was why Gemma went with her. Their sudden departure had made it appear that it was his fault.

He proceeded to crawl, painfully, upstairs. On the landing, he looked around the bannister to the door which used to be Gemma's room. His wife and daughter would laugh and chat together in there; and sometimes, Gemma would cry. John would listen to them occasionally and wonder what it was all about.

He crawled into his bedroom, shed his clothes and stumbled into the en suite bathroom. The powerful shower water fused with his dark yellow piss, and he squeezed gel into his hand.

Perhaps, throughout his life, he had had a sense, an intuition, that he was not experiencing life the way he should, especially when it became apparent that his new house wasn't satisfying him the way he had hoped, and perhaps this lack of connection with himself and other people was the reason why his family had left him.

In the bedroom, whilst drying himself, the phone rang on the bedside table: 'Yes?'

'Hi, John,' said Janice in her distinctively hoarse voice. 'I was wondering whether we could do something tonight.'

John shed his thoughts with a shake of the head and wondered what was wrong: 'Like a restaurant?'

'That would be nice.'

'Is it Philip?'

'I just want to get out of the house.'

John felt reluctant to go if Janice was going to talk about her difficulties with her husband all night, but he did also feel like getting out of the house which today was full of difficult memories that seemed to be dragging him down, on top of his amnesiac problems.

'I'll pick you up at 7 p.m. if that's okay?'

'Thank you, John, that would be lovely.'

'Shall I park up the street?'

'No, he won't be back until late.'

In the bathroom, he looked at himself in the mirror. His miserable head stared back, still suffering from a pounding headache. The lines of his cheeks and the cracks around his eyes were more pronounced than usual, and his hair, still a little wet from the shower, looked thinner than it did when dry, with noticeable bare skin extending further back over his skull. He tried smiling to practise his sensitive smile for Janice later when they discussed her situation with Philip. The mouth stretched normally, but something was wrong: it looked more like a grin. It extended outwards whilst his eyes remained cold: a sensitive smile required a collective facial effort. He looked away, composed himself, visualised Janice sitting opposite and looked back to the mirror. She was talking about her problems with Philip, and he extended his hand to touch hers, saying: 'It'll be alright'. He froze like a photograph and analysed the smile. His eyes were slightly squinted which made the mouth appear genuine.

In the evening light, terraced houses, stacked on the surrounding hills of Toxon, reflected a Martian hue. John parked in a street that faced downwards into the valley, walked up a driveway and knocked on number 24. Suddenly, he wondered whether Janice still lived here. Since waking in hospital, not once had he gone to her house or investigated whether she still lived at the same address.

'Hang on a minute, John,' a raspy voice said, behind the door.

He sighed and, half a minute later, the door opened. She looked casual and pretty, her auburn hair flowing past her shoulders.

'Where to?' he said.

'I thought The Fox and Hounds.'

He was glad she made the decision. If tonight she wasn't happy, then at least she couldn't blame him on the location. Perhaps his wife's old criticisms, however, were still on his mind – even after so many years – because he couldn't imagine Janice complaining about such things.

They drove along the top of the valley where peripheral houses obscured the view of the town below. On the other side, farm fields undulated beyond. In the pub car park, Janice was slow to get out the car so, to get her moving, John did the gentlemanly thing and opened her door. She smiled but did not say anything.

Inside the relatively old pub built of grey stone and slate roof, they were shown to their table and given menus. The décor had recently been refurbished, losing the building its old charm and becoming more like a restaurant catering for families. Two lads at the bar, who didn't acknowledge the new family-friendly atmosphere, were drunk and laughing loudly, irritating the barman standing opposite. The barman, short but stocky and also head of staff, ignored them, as much as he could, while he observed the new boy delivering consistent errors and sending dinners to the wrong tables. The new boy, probably straight out of school, adopted a careless approach to his new-found profession but, nonetheless, feared his boss. The combination of fear and carelessness – a lethal catalyst – resulted in a profound ineptitude: 'Useless,' the barman muttered, before directing his gaze back to the drunken wankers opposite.

John ordered the drinks as Janice sat, rather sombrely, opposite him.

'There are complications over the divorce,' she said, finally.

'I'm sorry to hear that.'

'Emma doesn't know yet. I hope it doesn't mess with her studies.'

Emma was her daughter. John moved his hand across the table, touched her arm and tried the smile he had practised in the bathroom earlier: 'It'll be alright. Things will work themselves out. Emma's got her own life at university now, so she won't be affected too much.'

Janice hummed quietly in agreement and looked away at another table. John followed her gaze. There were families at large round tables and young couples at small candlelit tables. One young lady and boyfriend sat close to a family that demonstrated a lack of parental discipline, with loud and unruly kids aiding confirmation of the young lady's ambition to become a better parent. Staring directly into her boyfriend's eyes, she applied a sterner voice. The boyfriend, sensing both her agitation and ambition and afraid of the road ahead, erratically twitched his right leg and restlessly moved his eyes, avoiding contact with hers and the family next to them.

John remembered wanting to live in the countryside away from people but of still not feeling satisfied when he did. After his family left him, he couldn't find satisfaction on his own, either.

'Have you got a divorce yet?' Janice asked.

He felt a little unnerved by her attention suddenly directed to him: 'No, we never got round to it. I still pay her monthly instalments.'

'Aren't you going to sort it out?'

John shrugged.

'Perhaps you don't want to let go,' she said.

John didn't know.

'Sorry, I shouldn't pry.'

'There seems to be a futility in wanting things to be better,' he said, by way of explanation.

Janice looked down at the table, slightly dejected.

'Of course, in your situation,' John said, 'things will be better when you get a divorce, because you're obviously having a bad time. But in my case, life seems to go on and on, and it doesn't matter what I do to change things because, in the big picture, things remain the same.'

He was surprised by the meaning and weight of his words. They were real and significant, encompassing the reality of all his life, not just the recent problems of his amnesia.

'Whatever happened to the person who designed the Zenith building?'

'What do you mean?'

'You seemed so changed during that period.'

John hadn't talked much about that time with Janice, because doing so would risk revealing his amnesia, and she had never intimated anything particularly interesting or surprising about that period. In fact, he had tried to imagine that period, himself, as if he could remember it, creating his own truth, but with little believable success, because he couldn't risk talking to others about it: 'How do you mean changed?'

'I don't know. I guess, enthusiastic about the building.'

John remembered the moments before he crashed his car, how enthused he was about the prospect of designing the next Zenith building before all this media attention and politics: 'Well, obviously, I was happy when working on the building.'

'I guess so,' Janice said, slowly.

John detected she was alluding to something else, something about him during that time, and he didn't want to let this opportunity go: 'I mean, you didn't see me when I initially designed the building, because I did it on my own at home.'

'But you did come into the office a few weeks later to show your designs to Pete, and you kept coming in afterwards.' She looked down a moment, remembering: 'Odd, it was, how you changed so much. I mean, obviously it was the building that gave you this new lease of life, but there seemed to be a real, deep-seated change in you, too.'

'How do you mean?'

'You're asking me as if you're not aware, yourself, or as if you don't remember that time or something.'

He smiled and shook his head to disguise his amnesia but wanted to be as truthful as possible to try to understand what she was saying: 'In a way, I don't really remember that time, because I don't have the creativity I had then. I can't remember how I was able to design such a building.'

'You feel your creativity has dried up?'

'I've tried to do some more designs of new buildings, but they're terrible. I need whatever I had during that time to find my talent again. What do you mean, you noticed a "deep-seated change" in me?'

She looked, contemplatively, down at the table. Her freckly features were not noticeable in the soft restaurant light: 'It's hard to describe. Obviously, you had more drive, more concentration and a passion for the building, which was easy to see, but there was something I detected in you that I don't think other people noticed.'

'What was that?' he said eagerly.

She shook her head: 'I don't know. Maybe I'm wrong.'

John leaned forwards: 'Go on. Maybe it's woman's intuition or something.'

'Well, I suppose, it was as if that underlying thing in you, something I've always recognised that seems to drag you down, was no longer there. You seemed to be... free.'

'Free?'

'Yes, even towards the building, itself. You appeared passionate and focussed, as I said, but beneath this emotion there seemed to be a carefree detachment in your approach to the building, almost as if you didn't mind whether you got the Zenith contract, and once you did get the contract, it seemed that you didn't mind what Zenith or the world thought of you. None of it mattered, and yet, on the surface of things, you appeared like a typical artist, passionate and driven. You were focussed, and yet, beneath it all, you didn't care. You were unlike anybody I've ever seen. The change was staggering but uplifting, too.'

Again, John remembered the moments before he crashed his car, of how he felt enthused about designing the next Zenith building, but he also remembered something else – something he'd dismissed since first waking in hospital. He remembered the absolute certainty of designing it, too: not just sureness in the normal way of being confident about achieving something in the future, but the unequivocal faith that he would be the next architect. It was a faith that was not propelled forwards by the motivation of fear but by the motivation of truth. It was a startling memory, and he had to pause a moment to remember he was in a restaurant, away from the fast-approaching bend in the night. Was this freedom the same freedom Janice was speaking of?

'I did feel free, I remember,' John said.

She smiled and appeared slightly sad: 'But, then, you had lost it when I saw you in hospital. Whatever you had was gone.'

John was a different person during the amnesiac period according to Janice. He was somebody who was 'free'. Was the amnesia and lack of freedom now linked in some way?

'Why haven't you told me this before?' he asked.

She shrugged: 'Because it's very hard to explain.'

The boy waiter, the one who was annoying his boss, arrived at the table with their drinks: 'Have you decided on your meals?'

They ordered, and the boy walked away without asking whether they wanted salad or vegetables, and chips or potatoes.

John didn't know what else to ask about that period without exposing his amnesia. What Janice had described was the antithesis of the man he was now and, indeed, the man who lived before the amnesiac period up until the moments before he crashed his car: a man who lacked the talent or artistic inspiration to design the Zenith building.

Their meals arrived with vegetables and potatoes, and they ate in silence. The hangover headache he had had earlier today was beginning to return, so he decided not to have coffee after the meal and neither did Janice. He paid for them both, and they walked back to the car in the night.

On the road, they remained silent until John realised Janice might not want to see Philip again tonight: 'I have a spare room.'

She turned and smiled: 'Thanks.'

He headed home over the dark hills.

As they had sex, John watched his shadow moving back and forth on the wall in front of him, made possible by the soft lamplight. She had asked him, minutes ago, whether he ever wanted sex with her again, and the news had shocked him. Apparently, they had had sex during the amnesiac period. With a wish to re-enact the scene from that time to try to jog his memory, he had obliged, and now he watched the shadow on the wall, as if it were the person then – during the amnesiac period.

Afterwards, with no memory having been triggered, he turned to Janice and noticed she'd snuggled down into the bed with her eyes shut. He remained sitting in bed, staring at the curtains in the soft light with owl-like eyes. The light from the lamp created shadows in their creases and, after a minute, he turned towards the lamp and turned it off. The room became black and, in the darkness, he remained still, thinking about the things they were talking about in the restaurant and wishing he could remember the amnesiac time again.

He carefully lifted the duvet off his legs and walked quietly across the landing into the study where he switched on the light. Next to the desk was the drawing board. On it was his latest attempt to redesign the Zenith building – a front elevation drawn in pencil. He had tried to be innovative, placing windows in obscure places and using a mixture of metal and stone materials. He'd tried to make it complicated, because he knew the real building was complicated and, with that objective, he had succeeded, but it was ugly and monstrous. The real building was, apparently, wholesome and beautiful, defying its complicated make-up. That much, he was able to know. Where was the real Zenith building now, and where was the person who designed it?

He felt a sudden inclination to go back to the crash site to see if he could begin from where his memory was lost and find that freedom again. He dressed quietly in the bedroom, crept downstairs, passed through the kitchen to the side door and along the short path to the garage in the cool night air.

The car moved tentatively over the gravel, up the curving driveway and through the iron gates. The plastic steering wheel, the rev-counter and the long green bonnet made him feel closer to that night already.

He drove through the bend and u-turned up the road, so he could approach it from the right direction. Like that night, the fields began to pass by quickly, the white lines in the centre of the road sped beneath the car and the dial on the rev-counter moved towards the red. The memory of the feelings he had experienced when he crashed became more mysterious with Janice's description of him during the amnesiac period. 'Free', she had said.

The bend approached, and he slammed his breaks just in time, skidding all the way to the edge and almost crashing again, but allowing the car to fall into the dip off the side of the bend where he had, so violently, crashed before. The car stopped, and his head slumped onto the steering wheel.

Six months ago, a few days after the meeting with the reporter at the Zenith offices, he had gone to his GP and ascertained that he had broken his wrist and suffered mild concussion from the original car accident. Then, he had gone to the Jaguar garage to enquire whether he'd taken his car there after his crash and learnt that he had. Their records showed the front of the bonnet had been crumpled with one headlight broken.

Janice's words tonight had made the fight for his existence now real. He believed in this freedom. This belief, however, was not enough to overcome the amnesia. He still felt the malevolent nature of the darkness in the slightly weird reality of the road, the fields and the room at home where Janice was sleeping. Indeed, he had often felt it, to a lesser degree, throughout his life, and it had returned to him on the night before construction began, taking the Zenith building from him.

This was a profound realisation: the darkness had always been with him, even before the amnesia. The amnesia and his blindness to the building seemed to be a direct embodiment of it: a vengeful theft of the potential John had achieved in the short time he had become free of it. Throughout his life, it had always stopped him from achieving his potential; and after he did finally overcome it for a short time, it had stripped his memories from him with that vengeance. But, in doing so, it had revealed itself. Its insidious nature had come out into the open in the form of his amnesia. But what, exactly, was it, and where did it come from?

To ask this question directly, or to stare at the building, would only give it another chance to destroy him. He feared he might materialise here to four years ago – or die! – or that anything might happen that expressed its ultimate wish to suppress his truth. It was his truth against its truth. He had to find another way of understanding it: perhaps by seeking what it denied – his freedom.

Indeed, where did his freedom come from on the night he crashed his car, and why was it taken from him on the night he tripped and hit his head? He sat in his car for a few more minutes, hoping these new questions might be enough to jog his memory of waking after he had crashed his car, but no images or thoughts came to him, so he drove back home and crept silently upstairs, avoiding the creaking floorboards.

The next day, when the sun pressed its spring rays onto the back of the curtains and made them glow orange, John listened to the humming pitch of a woman in his en suite bathroom. Such a rare thing, these days, to have a woman in the house. He remembered the sex last night and the freedom she said that he had had during the design process.

'What's wrong?' she asked, walking into the bedroom with a towel over her head.

He realised he was frowning and tried to smile.

'Gosh, don't overdo it,' she said. She seemed to be feeling better.

He smiled, genuinely this time.

'Last night doesn't have to mean anything, you know,' she said. 'Things can go back to normal, like last time. And I didn't sleep with you on the rebound – if that's what you're thinking.'

John shook his head and smiled whilst trying to think more about the significance of the moments before he had crashed his car.

9

In Toxon shopping centre, after having left the car park, Janice walked ahead to the office whilst John bought a newspaper and chocolate muffin in his usual café. In today's paper was an article about the upcoming Memorial Service for the 179 people who lost their lives in the terrorist attack. It was to be held in a couple of weeks outside the Zenith construction site, marking the four-year anniversary. The world's media would descend upon Blanworth, just as it had done in previous years, apparently. It was not without controversy:

'The upcoming Memorial Service has reawakened calls by the Muslim Assembly of Britain to both Zenith and the government for the resignation of Mr Wilkinson Junior, the son and employee of the Zenith CEO. It was Junior's disparaging remarks against Muslims wanting to retrieve land from the Israelis that incited the deplorable terrorist attack.

Shortly after the attack, the government took the unprecedented step of bailing out Zenith who were not insured for terrorism, lending funds to rebuild their head office. At the time, the Muslim Assembly of Britain, whilst condemning the terrorist attack, argued that our taxes should not be used to rescue the firm and that Mr Wilkinson Junior at the very least should resign.

Now that the terrorists have been brought to justice and with another anniversary looming, the Muslim Assembly believes it has more chance, with growing public support, to force Wilkinson Junior to resign.

However, yesterday in the House of Commons, the Home Secretary Patti Smith said:

"The government maintains its position that the decision for Wilkinson Junior's continued employment lies with Zenith, itself, but I personally feel that if he were to resign, it would be sending the wrong message to terrorism."

Nobody from Zenith was available for comment.'

John finished his muffin and walked to the office. He tried to go into the office regularly, keeping himself familiar with the progress of the Zenith building and remaining abreast of general finances, all of which he did without daring to concentrate on the design of the building, itself.

'Pete asked if he could see you when you've got a minute,' Janice said, sitting behind her desk and acting as if nothing had happened the previous night. 'I told him I wasn't sure when you were coming in.'

John dropped his satchel in his office and walked zigzag

through the employees' desks and drawing boards to the middle door on the side wall. The other two rooms were used for meetings and presentations.

'Yes?' a voice said, low-pitched and nasal in tone, seeping through the chipboard.

John entered.

Pete was sitting behind his desk on the other side of the room. He wore a pinstriped suit with thin lapels – only two centimetres wide – and a light blue tie that matched his handkerchief. His black eyebrows were freshly dyed and hovered above the upper, black rim of his glasses with auspicious anticipation.

Throughout the years, Pete had proved to be a first-rate marketeer: an essential part of being a modern architect. This was something which had seduced many customers, but something which John lacked. Pete was married to a lovely lady – his third marriage; although now, he was having an affair with a man. Mildly talented at designing buildings, he did have some creative flare.

However, now that he represented the Gowan firm in radio interviews and newspaper columns as joint architect of the Zenith building, Janice had told John that Pete expounded his contributions to the Zenith design with hardly mentioning 'John Gowan' at all: the prestige having certainly gone to his head. Pete would have been involved in later aspects of the building, once John had shown him the essential design, but only concerning minor details which any professional could do, and John felt Pete had now gone too far in interviews, exalting himself.

'Good to see you, John. It's been a while.'

John sat in the leather chair: 'I've missed you the last couple of times I've come in.'

'I've been at the site a lot. Have you been recently?'

Pete never asked questions about John's curious lack of interest in the building or the outside world: it didn't matter, because everyone now believed Pete had designed it, too. Zenith were happy for Pete to be the man in charge as long as somebody was doing the job properly.

'A little.'

'Do you like what you see?'

John was as blind to the building as to the plans – a fuzzy mess – so he stopped looking after a couple of seconds to avoid losing consciousness again. He told people he'd been inside the growing structure, but he never had, only ever walking around it or going in the Portakabin. A disturbing anxiety over the continuance of his problems threatened him most when he was on site, whereby his heart pumped far too much blood around his body, stifling him from concentration and the ability to converse well. He therefore never stayed for long and explained to Andrew, the Site Engineer, it was best to deal exclusively with Pete, so as to avoid lost messages and complications.

'I do, and Andrew seems happy,' John said.

'He never seems happy! But I know what you mean. Things are on schedule, and he's doing a good job. Our employees are doing a good job helping me, too.' Pete stroked the table agreeably with his hand. Its sensuous design was reminiscent of the curves of a beautiful physique.

'So, why did you want to see me?' John asked.

'Mann phoned me, a while ago, to talk about the 25th February and the television studio interview he wants from us this time around. Neither I nor you have ever done anything on live television before.'

Mann had mentioned a television interview for the anniversary of the destruction of the old Zenith building a few weeks ago. Gowan Partnerships were contractually obliged to help Zenith with the media on important occasions, such as the anniversary.

'Mann, however, wants only one of us to do it,' Pete continued, 'because he wants the other at the Memorial event in City Square at the same time, so he was wondering which one of us wanted to do it.'

John could see Pete's keenness for the television interview. Pete would take the limelight yet again in front of the media for being the architectural face of the Zenith building.

'Is it local news?'

'No, it's national, but it's the news programme Newsbeat which uses the studio in Blanworth, anyway, so there's no distance to travel. During the interview, they will ask one of us questions about the building's design and its progress, thus far, in construction.'

There would be a small chance John could respond to one or two questions satisfactorily with abstract responses but not for the whole interview.

'Wilkinson will be at the interview, too,' Pete continued, 'and somebody from the Muslim Assembly.'

'Perhaps neither of us should do the interview,' John said, not wanting Pete to be the face of the Zenith building on live television.

'Why?'

John tried to think of an excuse: 'There is a Muslim in the discussion which means there will be some political debate between Zenith and Islam. We may be forced to be on Wilkinson's side and become embroiled in Zenith's politics which is something we shouldn't be expected to do.' A good answer, possibly freeing them from the contractual obligation to Zenith.

Pete shook his head: 'Mann said Gowan Partnerships won't be involved at all in that side of the interview. All one of us does is describe the inspiration behind the building and how it's matching up to our expectations, now that it's in construction, et cetera, et cetera.'

'But, in recent radio interviews, you have said that we designed the building for freedom, so it may be hard not to be involved.'

'Freedom in terms of a free society and freedom from terrorism, but it was never meant to be a political comment in favour of Zenith and its business practices. We'll talk to Mann, though, if you want.'

John nodded, slowly.

'Mann will explain everything properly tomorrow at a meeting at 3 p.m. at the Zenith offices.' Pete paused, his mouth open slightly, waiting to say something more: 'So, would you think I can do it, since I've been dealing more with the building?'

John knew the futility of wanting to do it himself: 'I'll let you do it, because you're used to radio interviews, but you have to make sure you emphasize that I designed the building, too. I've felt a little uneasy with you doing interviews recently and not even mentioning my name properly.'

Pete raised his manicured eyebrows and looked down at the table: 'I'm sorry. I had no idea. I'll make sure your name is included properly in the interview.'

On the way back to his office – a distance of just a few metres – the colours and textures of the white drawing boards, the young faces of his employees and the cheap brown carpet seemed unreal, even malevolent. The air, too, seemed vaguely poisonous. He wondered what they all thought of him, coming into the office and not working on the building directly. In future, John would have to involve himself more with the building in innovative ways, because he needed to feel more connected to this world as the Zenith architect.

Protestors didn't get in John's way as he parked next to luxurious cars at the Zenith temporary offices. Cordoned off by security guards, they chanted:

'Down with Zenith!'

'Sack Wilkinson Junior!'

'The Palestinians have a right to their land!'

Some were of Middle Eastern complexion, and others were white. There were reporters and television cameras, too.

John neglected to look into the faces of any of them, not through fear but lack of interest or, rather, a distracted mind. Arrangements for the anniversary would be made today between him, Pete and Zenith. As things stood, Pete would be doing the television interview whereas John would be at City Square for the Memorial Service.

A tall security man escorted John alongside the curved mirrored building that gleamed in the evening light, and he held the central glass door open. In the reception area, the dingy light and eerie silence, after hearing the shouts outside, reminded him of last time: of how he had feared the newspaper interview. Now, he feared meeting Wilkinson for the first time: a man he knew exclusively from the amnesiac period. He'd seen him at a couple of Chamber of Commerce meetings before the amnesia and, more recently, from television interviews and newspaper photographs, though that was hardly a consolation.

The lift felt unreal. The grey metallic doors seemed to lose a kind of focus, so did time, itself, and he suddenly wondered how long he'd been inside. The door opened at floor number nine, and he stepped quickly across the threshold into the reception area. To his right, the same young, blond man as before sat behind the desk.

'Are you alright, Mr Gowan?'

'Of course, why do you ask?'

'I thought I heard shouting, coming from the lift. It has been known to get stuck between floors from time to time.'

'No,' John said, 'there was no shouting.'

'Of course.'

The corridor loomed into the distance as he began his trek. Like before, there was a feeling of unjustified space in relation to the size of the building outside as the corridor curved around the bend. The regal red carpet felt buoyant and out of keeping with the cheap white doors and greyish walls either side that had the cork notice-boards and bland pictures of vegetation. The darkly varnished door that he expected to see eventually appeared in the middle distance as before. As he approached and touched the golden handle, muffled voices emanated from inside.

'Gowan!' cried Mann, who stood in the centre of the room, holding a sherry glass and grinning broadly.

'Hi, John,' Pete said, standing next to Mann. His deep, nasal voice was, in fact, the opposite of Mann's powerful and relatively high-pitched voice.

John instantly felt indignant that Pete had arrived first as if he were the true representative of Gowan Partnerships. It was true that Pete did, naturally, liaise a lot more with Zenith and that he was the resident architect at the site signing stage inspection reports and what have you but, in truth, it should be John's job.

'Mr Gowan,' an American voice said, smooth as silk.

John turned with fright.

A small man with silver hair, blue eyes and an immaculate grey suit walked from the window that faced the city, around the large oak desk and held out his hand: 'It's been a while, hasn't it?'

John recognised him to be Mr Wilkinson and shook his hand with a smile: 'Yes, it has.'

'About a year ago in this very room, wasn't it?'

John pretended to search his memory for a moment, then nodded: 'I think it was, yes.'

'Or was it at the restaurant with Mann?'

John felt anxious and pretended to try to remember again. The other two men were silent and, in this short moment of quietness, he feared that Mann and Pete suspected his amnesia and had told Wilkinson who was now testing him, but Wilkinson then shook his head.

'No,' he said, pausing and sipping his sherry, 'I think you're right. I think it was here.' He exuded a calm, understated presence, but there was an inherent control in his demeanour which demanded courtesy and respect. 'Did you get mobbed by the protesters downstairs? I've been watching them from up here.'

'No, I managed to get through them okay.' John's throat was dry, and he gulped: 'How long have they been there?'

'Only today. I think they decided to begin demonstrating today, because it's exactly a week until the Memorial.'

Since waking in hospital six months ago, John had learnt that the annual Memorial Service, held in City Square outside the Zenith site for the 179 people who died, exacerbated tension in Blanworth. It was seen by some as a publicity stunt by Zenith to promote itself as a company representing the British people: a company that still refused to sack Wilkinson Junior and supplied equipment to the

Israeli military. This had led to the terrorist attack which protestors, nevertheless, deplored.

John, himself, hardly gave the issue much thought, because he'd been too embroiled with his own problems since waking in hospital: 'Can't the police move them on?'

'Of course. This is private property,' Wilkinson said, 'although it's not Zenith's property, of course. We've been in contact with the owners, and we all feel that it would be best to let protestors do what they want for a couple of days. The owners like the publicity, because they have other floors to let. Even bad publicity is good publicity, and we want to appear tolerant. Shall we sit down?'

The men gravitated towards the four leather Queen Anne armchairs situated in the centre of the room – a similar arrangement to last time. Although, instead of water and tea on the glass coffee table in the middle there was a decanter of sherry and finely cut glasses.

As John sat with the rest of them, he noticed the room appeared distorted and odd, like the last time, as if the regal red walls leaned inwards. On them were equestrian paintings of famous races and military charges, and at each end of the room were broad windows: one, behind Wilkinson's desk, facing the city, and the other facing the distant countryside where fields demonstrated the flatness of the surrounding area.

Mann poured John a drink, then picked up a sheet of paper from the table: 'Okay, gentleman. On the evening of the anniversary, there will be an event at City Square with hundreds of people, as has happened in previous years. On a constructed stage, on chairs arranged in a line will be the Mayor, the local MP, the Bishop of Blanworth, Gowan, a small selection of family members of the deceased, and whomever else, each having a turn to walk to the microphone in the middle of the stage to say a few words. Throughout it, there will be a huge TV screen to the side showing pictures of the deceased. Then, a short service by the Bishop will be followed by a minute's silence.'

'Gross, isn't it,' Wilkinson said, 'this outpouring of grief once a year. I know we're partly responsible for the publicity, but every year the Council makes this Memorial bigger and more political.'

'It'll be a logistics nightmare for the police, as usual,' Mann said, 'but they seem to know what they're doing.'

John had looked at Mann's profile on the Internet several months ago to make sure his title of Captain was correct. He had served 25 years in the navy, before retiring. His skills as an organiser and tactician had presumably attracted Wilkinson, in addition to his marriage to a family member.

'Anyway,' Mann continued, after a slight pause, 'John will be with me at this event whilst Pete will be doing the television interview.'

Wilkinson smiled and looked at Pete, evidently pleased with the decision that Pete was doing the interview: 'You will be talking to the television producer tomorrow. He will give you an idea of the questions you'll be asked, but I talked to him today, and here's a brief summary of the interview.

You will be questioned first about the building, including its design. Then after a television report about Blanworth, I, the Mayor and the Imam of the Mosque will be introduced into the discussion, during which you will have nothing to say, except answering one or two technical points about the building that may arise. We will make it clear that you are not affiliated with the politics in any way. The producer knows this and understands your concern.'

John's unease grew with the way things seemed in the room. He was losing a sense of familiarity with everything, including the people present, as if he didn't belong here. The elaborate furniture and equestrian paintings appeared threatening, almost as if the horses were intent on running over him, and the photographs of children on Wilkinson's desk appeared demonic with their wide-faced smiles.

'Will Dianne Fielding be the interviewer?' Pete asked.

'Yes, just like normal on television. She won't grill you, though, as she usually does with her guests. She understands you have no political agenda, and you will simply be explaining your building.'

Pete smiled: 'Okay, so 43rfv…'

Pete's words were becoming indecipherable, and John stopped trying to listen. Otherwise, he would be sucked into an alternative truth: the truth of not belonging here in this present time as architect of the Zenith building. But, as far as John could understand, Pete wasn't talking about the building, itself, simply the format of the interview.

'… then we will go into the studio,' Wilkinson said, 'and

tthgse e56gtre %£… you should wear a suit, similar to the one you're wearing now, although I don't think fgryt ert… you'll have to ask them when $3rfv…'

John perceived that the cause of his affliction now was his not doing the television interview. Pete's status as joint architect may have helped John in the interview with the reporter and over the subsequent few months, relieving media pressure and responsibility for the building, but now it was exacerbating his problems. Pete's status had been a temporary solution for avoiding the darkness that lay beneath John's problems, but avoiding responsibilities for the building and, therefore, not even trying to be his true self ultimately could not win.

As he pondered this, the room grew more oppressive in form, like a colour television switching to black and white, and he knew he couldn't continue life in this way, even if it meant risking exposure of his problems to the world. John would either get through the interview and succeed, thus making his just claim to be the Zenith architect a stronger truth, or he would fail and return to wherever the darkness wanted to take him.

All three men, he realised, were looking at him, as if waiting for him to speak, and he ascertained that one of them must have asked him a question.

'Are you okay, Gowan?' Mann asked.

He had to do this interview – impossible, though it might be. His mouth opened, but no words exited.

'Gowan?' Wilkinson said.

'I've been a little worried about him over the past few weeks and months,' Pete said.

'I'm fine!' John spurted, gaining excitement and confidence. 'I just realised, with no disrespect to Pete at all, that, really, I must be the man to do this interview. I know that Pete has had experience doing interviews and has been working as resident architect at the site, but I really must do it.'

John paused and held out his hands in a welcoming gesture, inviting them to his own understanding: 'This interview would mean a lot to me because, so far, Pete has been giving interviews on radio, and I think it's time that I remind people that I am the joint designer. I'd like to tell them my story of how I conceived it.'

John stopped and hoped he hadn't sounded too passionate or weird about this television interview, risking exposure of his desperate need to do it. There was silence. Pete appeared shocked and dismayed with his mouth half-open and his eyes, perfectly still, focussed on John.

Finally, Wilkinson sipped his sherry and then put it on the table: 'If you feel up to it, well, then you should do it, of course. But it's between you and Pete, surely.'

'Yes, I'm sorry,' John said, 'I should have talked to Pete earlier, but I hadn't yet realised how much I wanted to do it. You understand, Pete,' John said, looking at him, 'that I'd just like the public to know about me, too, because you've been on radio before and had a lot of press.'

Pete still appeared dumbfounded: 'Well, er, I...' He shrugged his shoulders and blinked a couple of times: 'As the junior partner of Gowan Partnerships, I don't appear to have any say in the matter.'

An hour later, after further, detailed discussions about the anniversary, both John and Pete left Wilkinson's room and walked the curved corridor to the lift in silence. They entered the lift, Pete pressed the silver button, and they began their descent. The plain, grey metal sides seemed utterly different from when John entered hours before. Instead of being claustrophobic and unreal, they appeared bright and exotic, gleaming with an intensity comparable to the sun's reflection on a hot summer's day.

Outside, the protestors were a lot quieter than before. A few were smoking cigarettes, others sitting. One woman shouted, 'Idiots!' as they walked alongside the car park. They got into their cars without saying a word to each other and drove away.

Despite Pete's obvious anger at John for changing his mind about the television interview, and perhaps also for the insinuation that Pete hadn't essentially designed the building – when John had said how he, himself, had conceived the building's design – John knew he had done the right thing. He knew he couldn't go on with life this way. Either, he would dramatically succeed or dramatically fail, but at least he was now willing to fight. As John drove away, he got a phone call from Mann, asking him if he wanted a chat.

'I hope I didn't step on your toes,' Mann said, sitting back with his pint in his hand and surveying the pub.

They were both sitting at a table next to a window that

looked out onto the same road that passed the temporary Zenith offices, just a few buildings away.

'I only phoned Pete first, because I assumed he would be the natural person to do it,' Mann said, 'seeing as you haven't done any interviews on radio and have generally taken a step back from Pete, on matters regarding the building, since construction began. But, of course, I'm happy you're doing it.'

John sipped his beer, his second already; he would have to be careful not to drink too much and reveal his amnesia in any part of this conversation.

'I talked to the television producer on the phone, just before I got here,' Mann said, 'telling him you will be doing it. As you know, you'll be answering simple questions that you'll recognise like the back of your hand, such as why you chose to design the building in the way that you did, and how the initial conception came about in your mind. For instance, how will you answer when the interviewer asks, where on the building eher hhdi 34run…?'

John began feeling light-headed and stopped listening. The brave enthusiasm of his decision to do the interview had now, predictably, turned to fear. How would he respond to a question in the television interview that may contain information about the building which he couldn't even hear? It was the same problem he had had with the newspaper interview. Only this time, it would be on live television, and he wouldn't have Pete to save him. Eventually, Mann's mouth stopped, indicating John's turn to speak.

'I think that's pretty easy. I know how I would answer

that.'

Mann nodded, slowly: 'Are you sure you'll be alright for it?'

'Of course. As you say, I haven't involved myself much with publicity so far, but that's only because I haven't felt the need, what with Pete doing it. But now, I think it's time to show myself a bit. The last time I was in the news was when I had concussion, and that was hardly a positive story.'

John remembered what Janice had told him the other night: of him being a different person and free during the amnesiac period. He wondered whether Mann knew anything about him from that time. They would have met during the design development stage: a time when the architect, after his designs are accepted by the client, periodically meets with the client or his representatives to discuss revisions, according to the client's vision.

'We liaised a lot before construction began, didn't we?'

'Yes,' Mann said.

'Did I seem different then?'

'What do you mean?'

'You know, different to now.'

Mann grinned and lowered his bushy eyebrows: 'What are you talking about, Gowan? You seemed like you.'

'Is that all?'

Mann laughed: 'You ask as if you don't remember that time. You seemed like you, but we didn't meet socially, like this, away from work, did we?'

John realised it was futile to ask any more questions about

that time. Janice had intimated that only somebody who knew him well could have seen the extraordinary change in him. Mann knew nothing about who he was then or, indeed, who he was now: a person with massive amnesia and an inability to see the building. If he knew, would he – and the television audience – see him as the architect, a man of genius? Or would they see him as a person incapable of designing such a thing?

Mann's facial features seemed to become strange and distorted; his moustache lay ominously beneath his nose, as if waiting to slide off his face like a slug and wriggle across the table into John's skin. The atmosphere of the pub seemed somehow strange, malevolent and unwelcoming. The long, shiny wooden bar, which had seemed solid and substantial when he first walked in, now seemed hollow, empty and fake, lacking any real substance. The ornamental fixtures on the walls, the hunting pictures, the barman, talking to somebody at the bar, and Mann's facial features all seemed to ally against him in an insidious way, as if each object offered an objection to John's superficial existence. What was happening to this place? Was it changing, or was John? Was John losing belief in himself as architect? Did he deserve to be here with Mann as architect of the Zenith building?

John had to leave, get away: 'I've suddenly remembered. I've got to be somewhere now.'

'Right now?'

'Right now,' he said, dropping his glass on the table, striding directly to the door and out onto the path.

The evening was turning dark, and the bright headlights of cars made sharp impressions upon the road, like a knife cutting through butter. John began walking towards the City Centre. Buildings grew in stature, and windows were lighted at random intervals. A few new stars shone in cloudless gaps, like glimpses of lost kingdoms. Peculiar eggy smells emanated from roadside drains, and all images and smells seemed to fuse together as one malicious embodiment.

He paused at the beginning of the High Street and looked towards the building site. Janice had made him realise the other night that the darkness, which lurked a hundred meters up the High Street, had been with him throughout his life, returning with a vengeance after he briefly overcame it to design the building. With this new knowledge, might he see the building? Might he see the freedom beyond?

Doubtful and desperate, he began walking up towards the site, passing the Town Hall and continuing until the line of buildings that was connected to the shopping centre to his right was broken by City Square. It was fully night-time now, and the open Square was lit by street lights: the way it had been when he came here the night he took measurements. Except now, the Square was overshadowed by a black, skeletal presence.

A figure was sitting on the black iron seat, facing the building: a gatekeeper to another world perhaps, to the world John couldn't remember. The tramp had been with him the night from when John had lost his memory and the night he fell at the site – both sides of the amnesia. The last time John had seen him, the tramp had said something that, seemingly, conveyed understanding of John's problems and had made John practically run away, but John was desperate now to rid himself of his problems so approached the tramp and sat down. The stench of old sweat was horrendous.

'Do you remember when I was here about six months ago? It was raining, and I thanked you for calling the ambulance after I hit my head.'

The tramp grunted, without looking at him.

'I then told you I was looking for a time behind the darkness, and I asked whether you knew what I was talking about. You said, "I do" with considerable ferocity, and it caused me to fall backwards. I then left you. But now, I'm asking the question again. Do you really know about my lost time behind the darkness? How could that be?'

The tramp remained still.

'Maybe you don't know, and you're just a lonely old man.'

A soft breeze passed through the Square, disturbing a trail of steam which rose from the ground a few metres away. Blurred noises glided behind them.

'But if you can't help me, I feel the only way to understand the problem of my building is to face it directly. With my friend Janice's words the other night, I feel I can confront the darkness. I feel the truth of existing during that time, of designing the building, can defeat its truth of me having not existed during that time, of not designing the building. It would defeat me if the world knew of my problems. That is certainly the threat I have felt whenever people start to suspect my amnesia, but if I get to the truth first, before the television interview, then I may be able to do something.

'Janice told me I was free during the design process: a freedom she had never before encountered in anybody else. Perhaps we all have this darkness inside ourselves, stopping us from reaching our true potential. I have become particularly aware of it because, for some reason, I overcame it briefly, for three and a half years, and designed a work of genius that I can no longer see. Now I must overcome this darkness again. So instead of turning away from it, as I have done the past few months, I'm going to stare at it and lose consciousness again. That is why I need you here – for you to wake me up after five minutes. Can you do that?'

The tramp looked at the bottle which John shook in his hand.

'You can have the rest of this if you wake me in five minutes when my mobile phone starts making a noise. If you cannot wake me, then I will have lost, or perhaps none of this world will exist any longer, anyway, and I will be transported back to the time I crashed my car.'

The tramp moved his head with dubious strokes.

'And please, don't start drinking my whisky until all this is over. Understand?'

The tramp's left eye moved left to right, then settled on John. He grunted an acknowledgement.

'That's all I need – for you to understand what to do.'

John set the countdown timer for five minutes, then looked up at the building and stared at it. At first he noticed the yellow light from the streetlamps on the shadowy skeleton. There were metal girders criss-crossing vertical girders at odd and complicated angles, and large plastic sheets covered parts of the middle. He tried viewing the building as a whole to see if he could truly see it, even at this early, undeveloped stage. As soon as he did this, his consciousness started to ebb, and he lost a sense of where he was. His heart began to beat faster and harder, and he realised that a great danger was threatening him. The building's skeletal parts began to circle into a whirlpool of debris and flooded his eyes with confusion.

Fear overcame him, and he tried looking away, but the confused configuration of parts streamed through his eyes and filled his mind. He did not know whether, in reality, he was still staring at the building or lying back on the bench with his eyes closed, but the building was now in his head, and he could not escape. It was inside him and invading his consciousness, deeper and deeper.

Words appeared to him amongst the maelstrom of steel and debris: freedom... freedom from the terrorist attack... The words began to separate and the letters within the words, too. Soon they floated away behind the debris, and everything began to get darker, until he saw only blackness ...

A violent force pulled his arm, and he opened his eyes with a start. Yellow light blinded him for a moment – a streetlamp – and he realised he was lying on the ground. A grubby hand was tugging his arm, and he remembered where he was and what he was doing. He must have fallen off the bench.

'How long was I out?'

'Five minutes, like you wanted.'

John tried to remember what had happened, but his heart suddenly beat extraordinarily fast, and he could no longer think properly. He lifted himself up and saw the tramp, already swigging the whisky: 'Give me some of that.'

10

The television studios were located not far from the city centre on the west side of the city, just outside the inner ring road. A road broadly circled the acre of land where, in the middle, a large square, white building loomed. On the front green, next to a small car park, a huge satellite dish pointed threateningly towards the sky, like an anti-aircraft gun. John stood next to it, smoking incessantly.

'Mr Gowan?' a soft voice whispered behind him.

John jumped and turned. A smartly dressed Wilkinson, with finely combed hair above his ears and piercing blue eyes, stood before him. Next to him was a tall, broad man with an earpiece.

'I'm sorry, I didn't mean to startle you,' Wilkinson said. 'Shall we go in?'

They walked through the electronic doors, and Wilkinson gave their names at reception. A short, fat man, who introduced himself as Rick and whom John realised was the producer he had spoken with on the phone, led them upstairs and into a room with seats.

'I hope you're not too nervous,' Rick said to both John and Wilkinson. 'Mrs Fielding will be coming in shortly and should make you feel at ease. Are there any questions you might like to ask at this stage?'

John wasn't really listening, and the rest of the afternoon went rather quickly. They met the interviewer, Fielding – a black woman who seemed taller in person than on television – and ate tea in the refectory. Wilkinson made a few comments about the interview, and John responded as best he could, but he could not stop thinking how easy it would be for his ignorance to be exposed by some awkward, direct question from Fielding, especially if John could not hear parts of the question. John had had a pretty good idea of the type of questions since the telephone conversation with Rick, and he'd prepared answers that he hoped would satisfy Fielding's direct questions which he wouldn't be able to hear, but Fielding was notorious for not letting her interviewees go until she got the answer she was seeking. Fielding would be using a picture of the future building as a point of reference, too: something which John would not be able to see.

The frightening prospect of defeat, of losing to the darkness and being transported away from this world, churned around his fearful head into the early evening. He could be living his final few hours. But he felt angry and stubborn, too: being threatened by something that had always stolen his talent and was now trying to take away his claim to being designer of the Zenith building. Being pampered by an attractive make-up artist was a welcome distraction, and both he and Wilkinson laughed a little nervously at trivial things. Wilkinson had his own problems: taking the risk today of defending his decisions on live television to keep his son in his employment while also maintaining Zenith's contract with the Israeli military.

As John looked at himself in the mirror, he noticed how much he'd aged over the past few months, but then he remembered the years he had lost due to the amnesia and realised he was comparing himself to several years ago. White hairs on the side of his head, a receding hairline and deep lines on his forehead all seemed foreign to him. He relaxed his face to lessen the cracks.

In the studio, black cameras faced the stage with wires leading out of their backs; big, chunky lights hung from a latticework of scaffolding above; and television people stood close by. On Stage 4, leather chairs surrounded a round glass table that reflected the blues and purples of the elegant backdrop. Fielding sat centrally behind the table, and John was to her left. John would be interviewed on his own at first, answering the questions without Wilkinson or anybody else there to offer a chance of diversion. Behind Fielding, to her right, was a large television.

As the make-up lady gave John some finishing touches, Fielding gave some final words of encouragement, smiling reassuringly at John – an expression she rarely used on camera and which did nothing to calm his fears. She knew nothing about his problems and would undoubtedly love to expose them, as any newsperson would if they suspected the truth. She had a long neck and a lengthy rectangular head that resembled a robot; John tried to amuse himself with this observation to ease his fears, imagining Fielding self-destructing on stage to his evasive answers.

The distinctive music of trumpets and timpani sounded from speakers somewhere in the studio as the opening theme to the programme began, and then Fielding started talking to the camera in her loud, authoritative voice:

'Four years ago today, the nation was shocked by the terrorist attack on the Zenith building where scores of people died. Police soon learnt that it was the work of British terrorists and, over the following months, an international manhunt was conducted.

'Three years later, those responsible were brought back to England and tried in court where they were found guilty and given life sentences.

'This evening, we will discuss the mood of Blanworth today, and our reporter Johnny Walker will also be reporting on the city's four-year anniversary of that horrible attack. In the studio, joining us later, will be Mr Wilkinson, the C.E.O. of Zenith, and Abdul Hassim, the Imam from Blanworth Mosque, discussing Zenith's controversial business practises, but first, joining me now, is John Gowan, the joint architect of the new Zenith building. Good evening, Mr Gowan.'

'Good evening.'

'Your building has been unofficially dubbed "The Freedom Building" by the media and the public in response to the terrorist attack, and its design aptly appears "free". Was this your intention?'

'Yes, the idea of freedom influenced the way I designed the building as a result of the terrorist attack.'

'And what does freedom mean to you?'

John remembered staring at the building in City Square a few nights ago. He had looked into it and witnessed a secret before the tramp had saved him from the enveloping darkness. The secret had something to do with freedom: perhaps the freedom he experienced when he designed the building. He couldn't remember. Whenever he tried remembering, his heart beat rapidly and his head clouded in confusion, akin to a panic attack.

'Freedom means democracy. It means the right to live in a fair and just society. It means the ability to live a lawful life without the fear of attack. On the day of the attack, our freedom was briefly shattered. I will never forget the terror, the sorrow on people's faces when I went to the Zenith site a day later and saw them gathered around a huge mound of rubble. Even then, I wanted to give something to Blanworth, to the people, to me and to everybody else. I wanted to design a building that stood up to terrorism in the name of freedom. I wanted to design a building that visually encapsulated the idea of freedom.'

She smiled and sat back into her chair: 'And you certainly did that! I would like to show our viewers a picture of the completed building.'

The television screen behind Fielding's right side suddenly lit up and, for a moment, John tried looking at it, but an image of bright colours and diagonal lines appeared which immediately became incomprehensible. He looked away and quickly recovered.

Fielding was staring at him with her eyebrows raised, and John realised she must have said something: 'I'm sorry, could you repeat your question?'

'Could you describe to us what we're looking at?'

John tried to remember the little he was able to know about the building: the abstract knowledge which revealed nothing of the building's actual appearance.

'My building', he said smiling, 'is something which I'm very proud of. As you can see, it is a big building, complicated, intricate and yet simplistic in its overall appearance. You see, the floors are arranged in a particular way to get the maximum use out of the materials, and –'

'What materials were used?'

'I would like to ask you – and the viewers watching – the same question. What materials do you think were used?'

'Well, looking at it, given that the colours are 765vfrt%£…'

John watched her mouth move and, for a brief moment, he tried to listen, but his consciousness, consequently, became dizzier, unable to understand what Fielding was saying. In the midst of light-headedness, he remained aware of what was happening to him and concertedly detached himself from Fielding's hypnotic sounds so that his thoughts would return clearly to him again.

'Mr Gowan?' Fielding said, suddenly.

John recovered instantly and smiled: 'I'm sorry, I'm feeling the effects of nerves on television!'

Fielding smiled, too: 'That's okay, television can be a daunting experience if you're not used to it. I asked whether

I was right about the materials.'

'I'm getting used to it, though, I think!' he said, trying to keep the conversation on the subject of his anxiety, rather than the building, for as long as possible. 'It just takes a little getting used to.' He paused and gulped, wasting a little more time. 'Anyway, in response to your question, you may well be right, you may be wrong, and there are some people out there who will know whether you are right or wrong, but I'd like the viewers who don't know to gain a natural curiosity for the building and discover for themselves what it is made of. There is plenty of information on the Internet. I'm speaking especially to those younger viewers who might have aspirations to be an architect one day.'

He turned to one of the television cameras, breaking protocol: 'Is Dianne Fielding right? Look at its colours, textures and size. Perhaps teachers at school might be inspired to do a project – not just of my building but of buildings in their environment.'

Fielding stared at him, clearly unimpressed with his answer, and John suddenly felt a terrifying loss of connection with his surroundings. The television studio became odd, almost disjointed. The black television cameras, with their transparent lenses, changed form in an illogical way: a way that he couldn't account for – as if they were replaced by identical cameras.

'You clearly don't want to explain the materials used,' Fielding said incredulously, 'but can you tell me what safety provisions are in place against another car bomb in the car park? Presumably, the materials will be stronger this time?'

The possibility of a car bomb, in Fielding's question, indicated that the new Zenith building had a car park, too. John had guessed the new building would also house a car park because, as with the previous building, Zenith required car space close to town. This knowledge, John believed, enabled him to hear Fielding's question without his problems stopping him.

'The public can be assured that this building will be a lot stronger and sturdier than the last. If the same were to happen again, which would be highly unlikely because of the new security provisions that will be in place, the building would not collapse, and all people elsewhere in the building would remain safe. The new building is designed in such a way that, if the worst were to happen again, its fundamental structure would not be affected.'

'What about a bomb going off in the shops on the ground floor? Couldn't somebody walk in with a bomb and blow up the building?'

As with the ability to hear about the possibility of a car bomb in the new building, John knew the shops would return: 'Assuming a bomb the size of the last one could foil security and get inside a shop, it would only make a slight impact on the building, because there is heavy protection between the shops and the rest of the building.'

Fielding nodded contentedly: 'Can you talk a little about construction now – is it going well?'

John felt a wave of relief spread through his body, now

that she had ended questions on the design of the building. She clearly didn't suspect there was anything wrong with him and was being less interrogative than with her usual political interviewees. The strange malicious objects in the room suddenly normalised again.

'Yes, it is. Everything is on schedule. If you were to go to the site now, you would see a lot of activity: trucks, cranes and, of course, the beginnings of the new building, towering into the sky.'

'That sounds exciting! Are you there every day?'

'Sometimes when there is a problem, the Site Engineer may need me,' he said, realising he was lying to impress, 'but Pete Williams, the partner in my firm, has been at the site far more than me, working on things. You see, I tripped and sustained an injury to my head the day before construction began, so Pete took full responsibility at the site whilst I recovered. Then we both realised he might as well continue, since he was doing such a good job – one person is better than two when dealing with contractors and clients. Otherwise things get confused. Meanwhile, I've been working in the background and doing other company stuff.'

'As he was the joint designer of the building, can you explain Pete Williams's contribution to the design? I believe he is attending the Memorial Service outside the Zenith site today.'

'He made some refined contributions to the design after my initial work at home – as did the rest of my office – but I was the one who conceived the building's overall picture, its look.'

'I see. And after you finished designing it, how then did you come into contact with Zenith, and did they change anything in the design?'

'Well, when looking for an architect, a company will send specifications to architectural firms, stipulating what it wants for its overall design. For example, how many floors, what size rooms, et cetera – not to mention the Council's requirements later. After I applied for the contract and successfully made the short list, I adapted my existing design to meet their requirements, but the essential design, its essence, remained the same.'

John's research of this period had enabled him to conclude that this was what must have happened. He had ascertained from Janice that two and a half weeks after the destruction of the old Zenith building, which was the time of his car accident, he had stayed at home for a further week and then returned to the office to show his initial design to Pete.

'And when is construction scheduled for completion?'

'In a year and a half.'

'Thank you, Mr Gowan, that's all we have time for right now, but please stay in the studio for further discussion.' She turned to the camera: 'John Gowan, joint architect of the Zenith building – in his own words. Now, joining us from Blanworth City Centre, just a mile away from here and where the Memorial Service is taking place, should be Johnny Walker.'

The television screen, which had shown John's

incomprehensible building, now showed Johnny Walker, a familiar reporter whose appearance was always dishevelled with loose strands of hair and a ruffled beard.

'Johnny, can you hear me?'

John felt a huge sense of relief and sat back in his chair, happy that that part of the interview was over without Fielding discovering any of his problems. Now he had to prepare himself mentally for the discussion later. Wilkinson and Abdul Hassim were yet to be interviewed, and John was still required to be present until the end of the programme to answer any technical questions about the building.

There were loud, echoing voices emanating from speakers, and Johnny Walker was smiling with his blond hair dancing in front of his eyes: 'Relatives of victims who died four years ago today are now speaking on stage to the hundreds of people gathering here in City Square. The atmosphere is quite lively and responsive – a celebration of the lives of those who died. But earlier, the occasion was far more sombre.'

Earlier footage of the day appeared, showing dignitaries on the makeshift stage in City Square with the incomprehensible image of the building behind. The dignitaries, one of whom was the unmistakable and colourful Pete, were sitting on a line of chairs, each walking to the microphone in turn to give a speech. Parts of the MP's and the Mayor's speeches were shown, and then that of a child of one of the security guards of the old building, wishing his father well in heaven. The next scene was of Johnny, interviewing the MP somewhere close to the stage.

'What do you see when you look at the new building?'

'Well, it's only halfway constructed, but it's already beginning to look beautiful, like the pictures.'

'Anything more?'

The MP paused and smiled: 'If you're alluding to its unofficial moniker "The Freedom Building", I see freedom, too.'

'And what does freedom mean to you?'

'To live in a democratic society of differing views, as long as those views don't infringe upon the freedom of others.'

'But what about some members of the Muslim community who think the Zenith building is becoming a symbol against Islam?'

'I find it curious how anybody could.'

'Well, Zenith haven't stopped their business dealings with Israel, and Wilkinson Junior is still in employment, despite his derogatory comments about Muslims wanting Israeli land.'

The MP smiled and frowned at the same time, conveying a bemused expression, as if Johnny wasn't making any sense: 'Do you really think the Mayor, a Muslim, himself, would be here, celebrating this day, if he didn't agree with this building?' He paused and sighed. 'Look, Wilkinson Junior, himself, apologised for his remarks, and many people, including non-Muslims, disagree with Zenith's business practises, but Zenith is a business and is free to practice within the constraints of the law. Anyway, this building is so much more than just Zenith. It's a symbol of the freedom of the society in which we live, and today it forms the perfect backdrop for Blanworth people to unite in their grief.'

The scene reverted back to Johnny – live – who continued to talk about the mood of Blanworth, and then back to him earlier in the day, roaming the streets, looking for people's views: 'Excuse me, sir. Excuse me, are you here for the anniversary today?'

'Yes. Me, my missus and the kids come to see it. We've been every year, so far.'

'What does it mean to you?'

'A lot. Our way of fighting terrorism, I suppose, and supporting the memory of the people that died.'

Johnny thanked them and moved to somebody else, asking the same question.

'Speaking as a moderate Muslim, I was horrified by the attack, four years ago today, and was further horrified by the news that it was done in the name of Islam. Let me tell you, this act was not the work of Islam but the work of a few deluded individuals.'

'What about Wilkinson Junior? Do you think he should leave the company?'

'Yeah. Personally, I do. But it's not up to me, is it?'

'But you're a taxpayer. The government saved Zenith, and so don't you feel you have a right to decide whether he should belong in the company?'

'Well yeah, but it's not like I can do anything about it. Anyway, I'm not here for Zenith. I'm here as a Muslim against terrorism and come to pay my respects to those that lost their lives.'

Johnny thanked him and moved to other people. After the interviews, the scene reverted back to Johnny Walker, live, who concluded his report.

Meanwhile, Wilkinson and Hassim had joined the table in the studio: the former sitting in John's old place, with John moving further away, and Abdul to Fielding's right. Behind Fielding's head, the television screen that had shown Johnny's report reverted back to flowing purple and green colours.

Fielding looked at the camera: 'I am joined now by Henry Wilkinson, the Chief Executive Officer of Zenith, Abdul Hassim, the Muslim cleric and Imam of Cromwell Street Mosque in Blanworth, and John Gowan whom I interviewed earlier.'

She turned to Wilkinson, holding a newspaper in her hand: 'If I may start with you, Mr Wilkinson. It was mentioned in today's Blanworth Express newspaper that some local Muslims see the new Zenith building, which is, albeit, still only halfway through construction, as a symbol against Islam and not a fitting backdrop to today's Memorial Service. What is your response to this?'

'Good evening. I would have to say, it would be curious to have a memorial service for those people who died without the site where it happened as a backdrop.'

'Some say the makeshift stage could have been positioned differently in City Square so that it would still have been close to the site but without the new building as a backdrop.'

'Well, then the location would have been less relevant and the occasion, consequently, less meaningful. But more to the point, in no way does the new Zenith building stand as a symbol against Islam. The new building is, if a symbol at all, a symbol of the free society in which we live. A society where we can practise any religion we please – Islam, for example – and rightly so. Today's anniversary was to pay respects to those who lost their lives on that tragic day – may they rest in peace – and if the backdrop of the Zenith building should mean anything at all, it should show that we, as a society, will continue to move on and not be intimidated by terrorists. An important message, I think.'

'But isn't it your moral duty not to keep your son in employment, in light of the comments he made six years ago against Muslims living in Palestine? And I quote…' She looked down at a piece of paper: '"Muslims go on and on about wanting to take back land occupied by the Israelis. But really, they should understand that it's not their land, and they have no right to it. In truth, they should be thankful for what the Israelis have given them."'

Wilkinson shook his head: 'Look, when he made those comments, his aim was to try to gain future contracts with the Israelis, but the Israelis, themselves, didn't like them. He was young and naïve at the time, and it was my mistake for letting him go out there. Believe me, I was very angry with him afterwards for saying such stupid things. He was sincerely remorseful and made an apology through the media, but unfortunately the dye had been cast and, a couple of years later, terrorists destroyed our building. I believe Zenith has suffered enough now and that my son has learnt his lesson. He has a heavy conscience and is desperate to do right by Zenith and the British people in the future. He's a valuable employee, and to sack him now would be just another victory for terrorism.'

'You say sacking him would be a victory for terrorism, but the terrorists have been brought before the law, tried and jailed. Therefore, surely, there is no risk of people thinking that the termination of his employment would be a victory for terrorism?'

'But we have already been punished by terrorists for his remarks, so to sack my son would be an extension of their intimidation, especially as he has thoroughly learnt his lesson and is profoundly sorry.'

'But your son's original comments offended Muslims across the world, many of whom also don't agree with the terrorist attack. To relieve your son of employment might, therefore, be seen as a kind gesture towards them.'

'I believe that my son's apology before the terrorist attack was sincere, and I also apologise on his behalf, right now, to all Muslims who were offended by his comments. But I also believe that Zenith has been punished quite enough so ask people to accept my son's apology as sincere and leave it at that. We are a company operating in a capitalist, democratic country and should be allowed to run things how we want – without outside pressure.'

Dianne Fielding turned to Hassim: 'Mr Hassim, surely

Zenith has been through enough, what with the terrorist attack? They don't need people telling them how to run their business.'

The Imam lowered his hand from his beard: 'Good evening. The publicity Zenith has gained since the terrorist attack has been huge and, although there was an initial drop in their share price after the attack, the value of the company has now more than tripled, so I wouldn't say that the attack was bad for business. As for Wilkinson Junior's comments, I believe he should be sacked immediately. Zenith is a large business which was saved by the taxpayer and, therefore, has a responsibility to do the right thing. So—'

'What about—'

'So I think—'

'Forgive me,' Fielding said, 'but what about the son's apology? Doesn't that mean anything to you?'

He shook his head and smiled: 'If he were sincerely sorry and had witnessed all the damage and death which he did not cause but triggered, not only to the people in the old Zenith building but in the Blanworth riots, shortly after the terrorist attack – not to mention the disturbances across the country – I think he would resign, or his father should sack him. Zenith has a responsibility to the British people, and—'

'But what—'

'May I finish?'

'Of course.'

'Zenith has a responsibility to the British people now that taxpayers have saved it from bankruptcy, so not only should the son resign, but Zenith should stop their business dealings with the Israeli military.'

'That's unreasonable.' Wilkinson said.

'Israel has continued to suppress the rights of Palestinians for decades and, as a British taxpayer, I don't think it is right that my money has, effectively, helped the Israeli government in their brutal oppression of fellow Muslims. Britain always turns a blind eye to what goes on there, feigning concern, and many people here suffer from a kind of blindness, because the truth hurts. Why is it that when Israel commits murder after murder, as shown on your News reports, the British government refuses to condemn Israel's actions? Is it because the British government was instrumental in creating the nation of Israel in 1948? This country suffers a kind of cultural amnesia, and the government should never have saved Zenith from bankruptcy without some conditions.'

'What conditions?' Fielding asked.

'The removal of Wilkinson Junior from Zenith and the halt in dealings with the Israeli military.'

'Mr Wilkinson?' Fielding said.

'First, let me say, Zenith is a business that has many dealings with many different peoples and companies across the world. The Israeli military is just one of many organisations we deal with, and we are just one business of many that the Israelis deal with, so it would be unfair to suggest that we supported them in their foreign policy. Secondly, when my son made those comments, he got a little carried away with himself on that day. He was young and didn't understand the true significance of what he was saying. His comments were not underlined by political motive – on the contrary. He was merely trying to gain favour and future contracts with the Israeli's. We are a business, and I personally regret any offence caused by his comments. As for the British government, I think it did the right thing in saving Zenith because, otherwise, our demise would have been a victory for terrorism. I don't think it would have been right for the government to stipulate conditions when saving us from bankruptcy, because then we would effectively have been controlled by the state – a state-run business – and that would have been a very bad day for capitalism. Something of which the terrorists would approve!'

'But you needed help from the government because your insurance cover for acts of terrorism had not been renewed at the last board meeting – as part of your policy to trim costs,' Dianne Fielding said.

'I don't think—'

'Also, the reason you were trimming costs was because, as shown in your figures at the time, you were already in financial difficulty. This meant the government saved you not only from the terrorist attack but from a demise that may have occurred anyway.'

'Regarding the insurance, I don't think anybody, in their wildest dreams, could have foreseen the attack on the Zenith building in which 179 people died. Regarding our financial situation at the time, it is true we were undercapitalised, but that was because we had made new, long-term investments and weren't yet benefiting from their rewards. The government knew this when they helped us. And, let me remind you, we have already started to pay back the government what it lent us – with interest – so Abdul's insinuation that his taxpaying money has been given to Zenith forever is simply not true.'

'I never insinuated that. What I am saying is, it is unethical to give taxpayers' money to a firm that supplies equipment to the Israeli military.'

'But, as I said, we do business with lots of companies throughout the—'

'And, I also object to the actual design of the new Zenith building, because it reminds me not of man's fight against terrorism but of the West's crusade against Islam.'

Fielding glanced at Wilkinson, then John and back at Abdul: 'How does the building's design remind you of the West's crusade against Islam?'

'The Christian connotations it has. Why, after a terrorist attack purportedly done in the name of Islam, would somebody design a building with Christian architecture?'

'What!' Wilkinson shouted, uncharacteristically.

Fielding glanced at Wilkinson, then John again: 'What Christian architecture?'

'Well,' Hassim said, holding one finger in the air, 'if we could look at the design again on the screen, I can show you.'

'Can we?' Fielding asked, looking to somebody offstage. An image appeared on the screen, behind Fielding and Hassim, which John didn't try to view.

'As you can see,' Abdul said, 'the uyter eruygg 4&*YGuI…'

John quickly stopped trying to listen to him, aware that he could not understand, because Abdul was talking specifically about the building. Dreading the moment they would refer to him as the expert, John wondered whether Abdul was correct: whether there was Christian architecture. It was a vague term, because many design features, such as gothic arches, innovations in roof design or even stained-glass windows – all of which were first created for cathedrals and churches in medieval times – were used in secular buildings today; therefore, the Zenith building may have ubiquitous features that could, arguably, be deemed as Christian.

'Mr Gowan?' Fielding asked.

John realised Abdul had stopped talking: 'Yes?'

'Is it true you had this in mind when designing the building?'

John tried to appear relaxed: 'No, it is not – in the sense that I didn't have any political intentions when designing the building.'

'I realise that,' Fielding said, 'and nobody here is suggesting you have any role to play in the political nature of these discussions. I merely ask whether you had Christian architecture in mind when it came to designing the building?'

'But Christian architecture is a term which suggests I wanted to put Christianity into the building I was designing. The answer to that is no. Firstly, I'm not a Christian—'

'And neither am I,' Wilkinson said.

'But Christianity is symbolic of the West's fight against Islam,' Abdul said.

'And secondly,' John said, pushing on, 'many design features that were first created for cathedrals and churches in medieval times are used in modern, secular buildings today. Therefore, the Zenith building may have such features, but in no way was it built with religious intention.'

Wilkinson nodded.

'But what of the iugIH *&Yv,' Abdul asked, looking at John.

John didn't know what to say: 'What of it?'

'Well, the JKhjkhb U7ybjh…'

John felt dizzy. He stopped listening and waited until Abdul's mouth stopped moving. Seconds later it did, and Abdul and Fielding stared at him expectantly.

'Well,' John said, trying to think what to say, 'it's inevitable that there are designs in today's architecture that originated in Christian architecture from earlier ages, and the same goes for Islam, too. Take the example of the gothic arch. It was used in Christian churches, but one doesn't necessarily associate it with Christianity if one sees it in modern, secular buildings. Anyway, I had no intention of designing a Christian building – Blanworth already has one cathedral and very close to the Zenith site. It doesn't need another!'

John spoke the last sentence with an air of authority, because he knew it would make him appear naturally defensive and bitter against Abdul's attacks on his building, and it might, therefore, seem unkind of them to continue questioning him.

'I don't mean to denigrate your building in any way,' Abdul

said, 'but I do take issue with a building that has Christian influences and is supposed to be symbolic of the West's stand against terrorism. That brings about connotations not of a modern country defending itself against terrorism but of an old Christian country crusading against Islam.'

'But the examples you use of the building's design are not valid,' Wilkinson said.

'I've heard other architects say they are,' Abdul said, 'and I can't say I disagree with them. Take the (*789hub, for example, the UIUYh& ...'

John stopped listening and waited for Abdul to stop talking, which he did almost immediately.

'I simply don't agree,' Wilkinson said, shaking his head. 'The (*76gbg Yygb...'

Again, John felt dizzy and stopped listening, desperately hoping he would no longer be involved in the discussion. So far, Abdul and Wilkinson seemed content that he wasn't commenting directly on the examples Abdul was using, but John feared that he would. He looked at his watch to see how much time was left for the interview – at least three more minutes.

Wilkinson stopped talking, and Fielding turned to the television screen.

'Well, as we can see here,' Fielding said, pointing, 'there is (*&69h IOUhgjb uhh... Would you agree, Mr Gowan?'

'What?' John said, looking up.

'Would you agree that, here, the UIgh *(&gH...?'

John had to stop listening. With so many words he

couldn't understand, he was feeling very dizzy. Fielding was now staring at him, her mouth frozen in the shape of a squashed circle. The studio began to appear threatening in an indescribable way, as it had done earlier. He was at risk of exposing his problems to the world.

'No, I can't say I do agree,' John said.

'But why, when—'

'I think he's answered your question,' said Wilkinson, who knew John didn't want to be involved in the political discussions.

John outstretched his hand towards Wilkinson in a gesture of agreement.

'But with respect, Mr Gowan,' Fielding said, 'you must have an explanation for your answer. It's all very well saying no but why "no"?'

The producer had promised John, before the interview, that he would not be involved politically with the others. Dianne Fielding either believed John's involvement was not political so could defend himself against Abdul's accusation that this particular architectural feature, whatever it was, was Christian, or Fielding just couldn't help herself.

'I think I've answered your question,' John said, repeating what Wilkinson had said.

'But if you cannot answer the question without explanation,' Abdul said, 'then it shows I'm correct about it being Christian.'

'No, you're wrong,' Wilkinson said and looked to John.

Wilkinson nodded to indicate John should answer

Fielding's question. John was very afraid and noticed that the appearance of the three people's faces seemed somewhat alien. Wilkinson's deep blue eyes and uncharacteristically anxious expression, Fielding's dissatisfied countenance and rectangular head, Abdul's great bushy beard and tensely stretched lips all seemed to threaten John's consciousness. He glanced down at the glass table with half-closed eyes to try to steady himself, before raising his head again.

'Well, broadly speaking, there are many architectural features derived from cathedrals that are not, nowadays, considered to be Christian in the slightest. Take the gothic arch, for example. In medieval—'

'You've said that. How about the example shown?'

Fielding pointed her thumb behind her to the screen, and Wilkinson looked at John with concern. Abdul began to smile, clearly beginning to believe John incapable of defending himself. All three people stared at him, the cameras too, along with, inside those cameras, millions and millions of viewers. What were they beginning to think? That John could not answer the question? That John didn't know his own building? That John couldn't even describe the intention of a particular design feature?

John could feel his fear – of the world discovering his problems – bulging inside him. His eyelids fluttered a couple of times, like a trapped insect trying to escape a spider's web. The light from the scaffolding apparatus above suddenly seemed to increase in intensity and heat. He glanced briefly at the television screen with the picture of the Zenith building and was tempted to stare at it to deliberately faint. The television screen, the people and the lighting apparatus began to move and to spin; images of spinning – of crashing his car into the ditch off the road – flashed before his eyes.

The moving stopped almost as quickly as it had begun, to be replaced by a terrifying darkness that flashed before him – on and off. Was he being transported back to that time – the aftermath of the crash – because he was unable to prove his worth as architect of the Zenith building?

'No!' John suddenly exclaimed.

'No?' Fielding said, eyebrows raised. She was evidently shocked, and so, too, were the others.

John desperately tried remembering the other night when he had stared at the building and confronted the same darkness. The tramp had saved him, but not before he had gained some kind of insight – some truth. His heart started pounding as it always did when he looked into that memory, stopping him from remembering properly, but his heart rate did not reach its normal level of intensity.

Suddenly, the words he saw at that time broke through and appeared to him again: Freedom… Freedom from the terrorist attack… And with these words, he made a mental breakthrough. It was so powerful and so profound that he forgot the need to be careful on television and spoke it aloud: 'You are all trying to find meaning behind the building,' he said in a steady, resonant voice in tune with his truth. 'Hassim is accusing me of its Christian connotations. Wilkinson says it portrays the freedom of our society – as do some newspapers and politicians – but the truth is something far, far different. Indeed, the very antithesis of what you think.'

There was silence for a moment, and Fielding then said: 'And what is the truth of the building, Mr Gowan?'

'How do you think the building was designed? Where do you think the innovation came from?' John asked, almost euphorically.

'You said freedom inspired you creatively,' Fielding said.

'Yes, but not in the way that you think! On the day after the terrorist attack, I went to Blanworth to survey the wreckage. I'd never seen anything like it, and I felt good from it. Something real had happened, away from the mundane experience of normal living. The people, the energy, even the air seemed different. Two and a half weeks later, this good feeling unwittingly had an effect on me as I realised, with certainty, that I would be the designer of the next Zenith building.'

People were looking at him, slightly gormlessly, not fully comprehending what he was saying.

'Many people see the design qualities of the building as an expression of the free society in which we live, but the great irony of the building – a building seen as a defence and glorification of our society – is that it was creatively inspired *by* the attack on our freedom!'

A sudden silence hit the room, as if a shock wave had passed through it. All people were looking at John.

'Are you advocating terrorism?' Fielding asked, finally.

'No! I'm just telling you the inspiration for the building's design.'

'But, you mean that the sheer horror of the attack inspired your design?' Wilkinson asked, looking threateningly into John's eyes and clearly wanting him to amend his comments.

'No, not the horror of the attack, but the freedom from the attack!'

'But what do you mean by that?' Wilkinson asked.

'I mean the way I felt as a result of the attack, and the way Blanworth appeared to me as a result of the attack. There was danger in the air, excitement, shock and, indeed, horror, but it was all free. For the first time in life, I felt free. Everything was suddenly natural and loose. Something real had happened, away from the contrivances of normal living. And with this freedom available to me, I designed the building.'

Wilkinson appeared shocked as he stared at John with eyes which weren't particularly open or closed but fixed and still, as if they had been stuck in ice. Hassim remained quiet but looked at Wilkinson with a smile. John realised he may have gone too far and damaged Wilkinson and Zenith, but he didn't care, because he felt that his new understanding of the building would reassert a connection with his true self and overcome his problems. Indeed, the threatening environment and consequential darkness had disappeared.

Fielding appeared shocked and said: 'I'm afraid, gentleman, time is up, and we are going to have to leave it there, unfortunately.' She looked at the camera: 'I hope you have enjoyed this discussion, and if you'd like to comment on our website, then…'

11

Wilkinson didn't speak to John after the interview: he simply walked to another room where he collected his things and left quietly with his bodyguard. John exited the building from where he entered it hours earlier and looked into the night sky. A cloudy darkness pressed heavily onto the artificially lit landscape below. He chose an arbitrary direction in which to walk – any would do – and proceeded. He felt a liveliness, walking the streets in the night, and remembered how, sometimes, the city's environment could become exciting and fresh: the way it felt when he first left the hospital several months ago and saw a future world for the first time. His phone rang.

'What happened?' Janice asked, her raspy voice unmistakable. 'Did you mean to say what you said?'

He smiled, as if she could see him: 'Do you remember what we were talking about before? Of how I seemed free during the design process, and of how I was trying to understand how I came to that state of mind which enabled me to design the building?'

'Err, yes,' she said quietly.

'Well, I realised the answer whilst on television, and I needed to vocalise it.'

He could see his darkness clearly in light of the terrorist attack. It had been with him all his life up until that point. It had the power to distort, suppress, manipulate reality and do all kinds of things that denied him his true self. It was a lack of meaning, a conflict, an unreal reality that thrived in society and in his soul. To identify the darkness specifically was impossible, because its identity was built on untruth and delusion – a symptom of the human condition; nobody was to blame; everybody was to blame. But whatever it was that had been inside him, inside his brain, inside his soul and perpetuated by society was obliterated by the attack on this society. The attack offered a doorway, a separation, a realness from the oppression at hand and, with this attack, his true self came forth to design the building.

'I realise it was a stupid thing to do,' he said, 'but, at the same time, with everything that was being said about the building, I believed the world needed to know the truth.'

'They certainly know now. The Internet is going crazy with people commenting on what you said. Zenith may well retaliate, although I don't think you said anything slanderous, because you only told the truth, despite the fact you changed your mind from saying the freedom of this society influenced your design, at the beginning of the interview, to saying it was the freedom from the attack.'

'You're the one with the law degree.'

'However, they still may retaliate in some way, so we're going to need to be prepared for the consequences. Do you understand?'

He tried listening and looked into the night sky, remembering the beginnings of the freedom he had felt on the night he crashed his car: of the fast road and the black fields rushing by. It was triggered by the terrorist attack, and the building's design was its manifestation.

'John?' she said.

'Yes,' he said dreamily.

'What did Wilkinson say to you after the interview?'

'Nothing. He just walked out.'

'John, I think, for the sake of redeeming your professional reputation at the very least, you're going to need to be publicly apologetic for the way you surprised everybody at the end of the interview. I will draft a letter tonight, explaining how you were nervous on television and shouldn't have said what you said in such a way.'

John waited at a road for two fast Saturday night cars to pass: 'Just as long as it's clear that I'm not going to go back on what I've said now.'

'What?' Janice asked, 'There's noise your end.'

The cars turned a corner, and John proceeded over the road: 'I said to write the letter, explaining how sorry I am, but I'm not going to go back on what I said.'

'No, I understand that, and I wouldn't legally recommend it, either,' she said with a soft voice. 'So, please come into the office tomorrow morning when I'll have your letter for Zenith, and we can take it from there. I'm sure they'll contact you soon.'

John continued walking with careless abandon. He didn't

care about the negative consequences of his actions; he'd found the truth behind the building, and he was enjoying the walk in the night. He ventured towards the centre of town and arrived at the Cathedral Close wall – a medieval construction of stone boulders, about six feet high. The back of the cathedral, supported by its buttressed exoskeleton, loomed large behind it. He passed beneath a Norman gate onto a gravel path, which edged the green in front of the cathedral's West Face, and through another Norman gate into City Square. Beer cans, napkins and cigarette ends littered the place – all leftovers from the day's anniversary. With no ignorance or anxiety as to how he came to design it, he looked at his building, expecting to see it.

At first, the construction seemed ordinary. There were upward shafts, horizontal shafts and sheets of plastic covering large sections. However, as he tried to ascertain exact materials, shapes and dimensions, the building immediately appeared shrouded in its own fuzzy haze – its lines and angles barely distinct from one another. As he stared harder, the whole structure began to circle in a vortex of confusion. A central blotch of darkness, like the eye of a storm, appeared before him, growing with considerable rapidity and flooding his eyes with confusion.

Fear overcame him like last time, and he realised his mistake; he tried looking away, but the blurry configuration of parts streamed through his eyes and filled his mind. He didn't know if he had fallen to the ground or was still standing, but the building was now in his mind, and he could not get away. It was inside him and invading his consciousness, deeper and deeper. Its parts began to break up, moving left, right and away in all directions, until there was nothing to see except darkness…

A violent force yanked his upper body, and he opened his eyes to see a man looking down at him.

'John!' the man said, his voice nasal and deep.

John tried to think, remember where he was. He was lying on the ground, looking up. The man staring at him was dressed in a colourful suit, and John realised it was Pete. He remembered staring at the building, and it then entering his mind. He must have fallen down. The building had fragmented, and a formidable darkness had appeared, similar to last time, except he hadn't seen the words 'freedom from the terrorist attack': words that were no longer consigned to the unconscious, perhaps.

He felt embarrassed, like a schoolboy who had been acting too arrogantly and was suddenly reprimanded by a teacher. He'd overcome a psychological barrier, but now that a gate had been opened, enabling him to know that it was the freedom from the attack that had empowered him to design the building, he realised there were still things to understand before he had a chance of overcoming the darkness. For instance, why did it return on the night before construction began?

Pete adjusted his glasses with his forefinger between the eyes: 'Are you drunk?'

John brushed his trousers with the back of his hand and

stood: 'No, I'm not. I just tripped.'

'Again?'

'Yes, and I didn't feel like getting up. I should never have done that interview.'

He was lying: he was glad he had told the world the truth.

'You think! You know you've just created a shitstorm for us, don't you?'

'I wanted to tell the truth.'

Pete raised his manicured eyebrows: 'By saying you were inspired to design the new building by the freedom you felt from the attack on the old one?'

'I was telling them the truth of how I came to design the building.'

'Well, there are two of us, as if you didn't remember. And why did you say I didn't design the building?'

'I didn't.'

'By implication, you did. You said everything was essentially your design and that you went to the office, after a week of designing it at home, to let me and the team work on the finer details. That doesn't sound like I jointly designed the building.'

'Well, isn't that the way it happened?'

'If you're going to name somebody joint architect, John, then stick to it, right?' He paused and stared at John: 'I've just been to the cathedral with Mann. He's praying. Praying! I never took him for a religious soul. We both watched a repeat of the interview on his laptop and, frankly, the words that came out of his mouth were not complimentary of you.

He told me to tell you – he didn't want to phone you himself – to go to Wilkinson's office tomorrow for a meeting at 10 a.m. Okay? I will be going too.'

John comprehended the need to help Zenith the best he could: 'I know I need to make amends. I've talked tonight to Janice who said she's going to write me a letter of apology to Zenith.'

He sighed: 'That's a start.'

'But, of course, I can't go back on what I've said – not after such a passionate revelation on television.'

Pete looked at him incredulously.

'Anyway, I'm tired, and I need to get home.'

The two men walked quietly through the shopping centre and into the multi-storey car park. After a long silence in Pete's car, John got out at the station and bought a ticket to Toxon. On the train, as he stared through the windows into the black night, he wondered about the nature of his freedom during the amnesiac period, also the other freedom – the freedom of society – and how the two were opposed. He had felt free after the attack on society's purported freedom. He pondered this for several minutes, until the lights of Toxon rushed by the window in a sudden whoosh and people began to stand in preparation to get off. He followed them through the station, out into the night, and decided to go to the office before going to his car: his laptop was there, and he wanted to watch a repeat of the interview in preparation for the meeting with Zenith tomorrow.

In the lobby, a familiar Syrian cleaner was hunched over a

bucket of water: 'Shame on you, Mr Gowan, for saying the things you did.'

'What do you mean?'

She stared at him with pained eyes: 'For telling people you felt free from the terrorist attack which inspired you to design the new building.'

'It was the truth.'

'Truth or not, I came to this country from war. I value its freedoms. What do you value?'

He didn't know how to answer her and walked into the lift. As it rose, a growing sense of guilt overcame him. What had he done tonight? What had he done to the people of Blanworth, Toxon and beyond who looked to the new Zenith building as a symbol of hope?

Toxon lights illuminated the main office with yellowy white rays, glinting off computer screens. In the shadows, he passed desks and unlocked the door to his private office. On the Internet he went to tonight's entire interview:

'...but first, joining me here is John Gowan, the joint architect of the new Zenith building. Good evening, Mr Gowan.'

'Good evening.'

'Your building has been unofficially dubbed "The Freedom Building" by the media and the public in response to the terrorist attack, and its design aptly appears "free". Was this your intention?

'Yes, the idea of freedom influenced the way I designed the building as a result of the terrorist attack.'

'And what does freedom mean to you?'

'Freedom means democracy. It means the right to live in a fair and just society. It means the ability to live a lawful life without the fear of attack. On the day of the attack, our freedom was briefly shattered. I will never forget the terror, the sorrow on people's faces when I went to the Zenith site a day later and saw them gathered around a huge mound of rubble. Even then, I wanted to give something to Blanworth, to the people, to me and to everybody else. I wanted to design a building that stood up to terrorism in the name of freedom. I wanted to design a building that visually encapsulated the idea of freedom.'

She smiled and sat back into her chair: 'And you certainly did that! I would like to show our viewers a picture of the completed building.'

His laptop showed a full screen image of the building, and he looked away immediately but, later in the interview, he would remember the words that appeared to him when he stared at the building: Freedom… Freedom from the terrorist attack…

He forwarded the recording to near the end of the interview. On the screen he looked animated – almost mad – with wide eyes gleaming and arms spread wide:

'Many people see the design qualities of the building as an expression of the free society in which we live, but the great irony of the building – a building seen as a defence and glorification of our society – is that it was creatively inspired *by* the attack on our freedom!'

It felt right to say this at the time – he knew it in his bones – but what did he really mean by it? What, exactly, did he not like about the freedom of this society? He continued to talk on the screen:

'Something real had happened, away from the contrivances of normal living. And with this freedom available to me, I designed the building.'

And why, on the night before construction, did he lose this freedom and confront the darkness of life once more? What sickness, what untruth facilitated the conditions for the re-emergence of the darkness?

He suddenly remembered something: on the day he awoke in hospital, he learnt that on the previous night at the site he had been holding a newspaper with a picture of the future building and the headline 'The Freedom Building'. The article praised the design of the building: a design that it said reflected the 'freedom of society'. The design of the building, however, had been inspired by the attack on society when its 'freedom' had been briefly obliterated. Had the irony of the article become too much when he saw how the expression of his freedom would be used to advertise the opposite?

12

John opened his eyes. The room was light – daytime already. It had to be eight or nine. There were faint voices from inside the main office. He placed his hands on his desk, heaved himself up and walked around his desk to the door. But, just as he was about to open it, he heard his name angrily mentioned, so he pressed his ear to the wood.

'But how could he say such a thing! On national television!' a male voice asked.

'Why would he? What was the purpose of it?' Another male voice said.

'I don't know.'

John put his hand to his head, remembering the truth about the building and telling it on television. What were people now saying? He put his ear back to the door. Both voices were vaguely recognisable.

'Pete should have done it,' said voice A.

'He would have done a lot better job. That's for sure.'

'John was embarrassing. I felt embarrassed in front of my kids.'

'Must have been nerves.'

'Maybe.'

'What do you mean?'

'I don't know,' said voice A. 'All that stuff he said about how freedom from the terrorist attack enabled him to design the building. It sounded like he was praising the terrorists and – I don't care how nervous he was – he wouldn't have said something like that if he didn't mean it.'

'But didn't he explain he wasn't praising the terrorist attack?'

'Well, whatever he was trying to say, it seriously embarrassed us and Zenith, not to mention the government.'

'Sure, but it was rooted in some kind of truth, because he did design it, after all.'

'Are you sure about that?' asked A.

'What do you mean?'

'Well, he's never really been involved in the building, has he? I mean, he's supposed to have designed it, but did you notice how, last night, he never really answered anything specific about the building, itself, almost as if he couldn't? And he hardly ever goes to the site, not since construction began anyway, like he's not interested.'

'But that's because Pete began the job on day one of construction when John was in hospital, and the two didn't want to get in each other's way later, so Pete kept the responsibility.'

'That's the official explanation, and that may be true, but I always thought it was weird how he announced that Pete jointly designed the building a few days into construction,' said A.

'How so?'

'Well, why hadn't he and Pete both said that they were joint architects up until that point? Why hadn't Pete said something until then?'

'Perhaps John was being kind when he named Pete joint architect – as a thank you for taking over duties on construction when he was in hospital, and for simply being partner in his firm.'

'Or perhaps John had been exploiting his position – as Senior Partner in the firm –over Pete until then, and Pete had finally had enough, forcing him to tell the world the truth.'

'But John conceived the initial idea of the building at home and then brought the design to the office.'

'Did you see the design at that stage?' said A.

'No.'

'So how do you know the final design was anything like the original? He supposedly brought the plans here for Pete to see. Then we all worked together on the finer details before sending them to Zenith. But, after John initially brought the plans to the office, Pete worked on his own for a while before we saw anything.'

'That's true.'

'So maybe the design was basically Pete's, influenced only by John's initial enthusiasm to design a new Zenith building, and it was this design which we all then, first saw and worked on.'

'Well, whoever designed it was a fucking genius,' said B.

'Yep.'

'Hi, guys,' Janice said.

John backed away from the door. Many things had been said in that short conversation. The television interview had certainly provoked them into sharing their derogatory views about him, and he understood why they might not believe that he had designed the building: Pete having looked at John's plans on his own for several days before they were shown to the rest of the office, and Pete working as the resident architect at the site since construction began.

John's mobile started ringing, and he darted further away from the door, hoping the two voices didn't hear it: the idea of him being an eavesdropper, in addition to the disreputable things they were saying about him, wasn't pleasant. Janice's name flashed on the screen of his phone.

'Hello, Janice.'

'Are you in your office?' she said, confused.

'Yes, I'm here.'

There was a pause with muffled talking in the background.

'The others didn't know you were here,' she said. 'Have you been here all night?'

'Why do you ask?'

'Your blinds are shut.'

'Would you get me a cup of coffee, please?'

'I thought that would never be part of my job description?'

John smirked: 'Just this one time?'

She ended the call, and John walked back to the door, waited a few seconds and opened it. He rubbed his eyes to show his employees that he had just woken up and noticed the fearful faces of voices A and B. He barely recognised them but stared at them with a disdainful expression, knowing it wouldn't be a bad thing if they suspected he had heard their conversation: fear of losing their jobs would prevent further gossip about him. They quickly looked away and walked to their desks. Janice brought coffees from the machine, picked up a piece of folded paper from her desk and followed John into his office.

'This is the letter,' she said, standing beside him at his desk.

John slurped his coffee and opened it:

'Dear Mr Wilkinson

I deeply regret any offence that may have been caused during the television interview of [date].

I can only attribute any indiscretion to nerves: it being my first time on television.

Please accept my apologies and any reasonable help in rectifying problems that may have been caused as a result.

Yours sincerely

John Gowan'

'Short and sweet,' John said.

'I had written a longer letter, but I thought it best not to say much until we see what Zenith want to do.'

'I like the word "reasonable". I'm willing to help them, but I won't publicly change my mind about the inspiration for the building's design.'

Janice nodded slowly: 'You have to be careful, though. Zenith is a wounded beast, and the government will be behind them.'

His mobile began ringing: 'Hello, Captain.'

'Gowan, there's a meeting today at 10 a.m. – Wilkinson's office.'

'Pete told me last night. I'm sorry about the interview. I was nervous.'

'Yes. Well, we have to discuss how best to rectify the situation. We'll have our public relations woman with us.'

'I'll do my best to help. How's Wilkinson today?'

'He's calming down, in his own way. Anyway, see you then.' The call ended abruptly.

'That was Mann. There's a meeting this morning. There will be a PR person, apparently.'

'For what it's worth, you shouldn't be made to feel ashamed of what you said on television. They asked you to do the interview, and they should never have put you in that position if they weren't prepared for you to answer in a truthful manner. This whole thing is political.'

'Thanks. To be honest, I'm glad things have turned out this way. I needed to tell the public the truth.'

She nodded with a smile: 'Good then.'

A few days ago in the restaurant, she had said that he was 'free' during the amnesiac period, and his explanation last night of where his freedom came from must have interested her. He suddenly felt inclined to tell her that he had amnesia and an inability to see the building. She might understand that all this was a problem connected to the conception of his building and that all he had to do was convince the world of where the building's inspiration originated.

But, for this reason, the darkness was still a threat. Until the world knew the truth – until it believed John – the darkness still had a claim to that truth and could easily have devoured him last night when he looked at the building, were it not for Pete yanking his arm. Who knows what it would have done with him?

'Time's moving on,' she said. 'You'd better go to this meeting now.'

John signed her letter, put it inside an envelope, which he marked 'Mr Wilkinson', and walked into the main office. Voices A and B were guiltily silent at their desks and pretended not to notice him.

'Is Pete in?'

They shook their heads sheepishly.

He tried Pete's mobile, but there was no answer. He and Pete needed to deliberate some kind of strategy together before going into the meeting. Pete needed to understand, in absolute terms, that John wouldn't refute anything he had said on television. John strode through the office like a wildcat marking its territory, pushing the door noisily into the corridor with a slap of his hand.

When John got to Blanworth Station, Pete answered his mobile.

'We should meet before we go into Zenith,' John said.

'Well, actually, I'm already in Wilkinson's office with the others.'

'What?'

'I was at the building site and wasn't needed there, so I

drove here early, and they let me in. Where are you?'

'I wish you'd talked to me before you went in.'

'Why?'

'Because we need to work out a common strategy.'

'I've told them you want to amend the situation as best you can.'

'Yes, but I can't go back on what I said, either.'

There was a pause.

'Well, we can hear what they want to do, then we can talk privately before coming to a decision,' Pete said.

John sighed: 'What's being said now?'

'They're just going over a few ideas.'

John quickly got a cab. He was angry Pete was there without him and feared them denigrating him behind his back. But Pete was angry with John, not just for embarrassing Zenith and Gowan Partnerships but for implying on television that Pete didn't design the building. Perhaps this was Pete's way of getting back at him.

He arrived at the semi-circular, mirrored building and rushed across the car park where protestors were camped next to the main entrance. Inside, a security guard, wearing a suit and an earpiece, allowed him through. The lift seemed to take a very long time, during which John's facial muscles stiffened uncontrollably. When the door finally opened, he walked straight through the initial reception area and down the long corridor that, as on both other occasions, seemed overly long, disappearing around a distant corner. The words 'Go ahead, Mr Gowan' were said by someone at reception, possibly the blond man who was there last time.

A minute later, or so it seemed, the darkly-stained wooden door appeared in the distance and, when he got there, after what seemed an eternity, he pushed it open by way of the golden knob. In the middle of the room, four leather armchairs were arranged around the coffee table like last time, but in-between two of them was an additional, small grey plastic chair. Mann looked up from one of the leather chairs and stood, as if to attention. John felt like he had entered a military court and was about to be court-martialled.

'Gowan,' Mann said smiling.

John walked between the empty, grey plastic chair and a leather chair that was occupied by Pete. The other two were occupied by Wilkinson and an unfamiliar woman with a frizzy hairstyle, wearing a grey suit.

'May I introduce Stacey Turner, our PR lady,' Mann said, gesturing towards her.

Stacey stood and shook John's hand whilst giving a condescending grin, whereby the mouth stretched outwards but the eyes relaxed deeply into their sockets. Wilkinson remained seated, looking calmly up at John.

John felt very uncomfortable. He remembered the letter Janice had drafted for him and fumbled about inside his pocket: 'Hello, sir. Here is a letter of apology which you may like to release to the press.'

John immediately regretted calling him 'sir' and felt like a schoolboy.

'I thought of that,' Stacey said, 'and drafted one, myself,

from you to Zenith, which could be shown to the media, but we won't be needing it now if you are willing to agree to our new strategy on how to deal with this problem.'

John nodded, and Stacey and Mann sat back down. Pete watched John with the faintest of smiles as John sat down on the grey plastic chair. Wilkinson remained quiet.

'Well,' John said, looking at Wilkinson whose silver-grey hair shone radioactively beneath the ceiling light, 'I am truly sorry for what happened last night. I didn't mean to cause any problems.'

Wilkinson lifted his hands and nodded: 'I know how you must feel, and I'm sure you wish you hadn't said it. Apology accepted.'

John did, actually, feel a little better, although he feared how they would react, once he told them he couldn't refute anything he had said: 'Thank you.'

'We've come to the conclusion, with the help of Stacey, that a radio interview, here in Blanworth, would be best to remedy the situation,' Mann said. 'We've been in contact with Radio Blanworth, and they are very willing to get their woman Rachael Haas from London to interview you tonight at 8 p.m.'

John felt panic and fear but tried to keep his composure: 'Presumably, you want me to downplay what I said last night, attributing my explanation as to how I designed the building to nerves?'

'Yes, you can certainly say nerves played a role in your behaviour, but it would be unwise to change your statement about how you found inspiration to design the building, because it would appear that we coerced you into saying it.'

A sudden wave of relief overcame John. His fears this morning of having to refuse their wishes were abated. The world would listen to his fuller explanation on the radio without any conflict with Zenith. But what did Zenith hope to achieve?

'So, what's the plan?' John said.

Pete looked at John with a sympathetic expression: 'I will counterbalance the importance of your words last night by reminding the audience that I designed the building, too.'

'You're going to be at the interview, too?' John asked.

'Pete will emphasize how he helped to design the building,' Stacey said, 'enabling the listener to realise that half the inspiration came from him. Of course, you will explain how it wasn't your intention to seem to side with terrorists in any way – because some newspapers today are interpreting your words as being sympathetic to terrorist attacks – but, in addition to that, Pete will help, too.'

'But will Pete explain how he found inspiration for the building the same as I did – from the destruction of the previous building?' John said.

'Certainly not!' Stacey exclaimed, and all the men shook their heads in unison. 'Pete will tell his side of the truth and explain how he found inspiration from the 'free society' in which he lives.'

The environment seemed malevolent as John felt the sensation of the walls beginning to close around him, but the darkness had been detectable since last night when he had looked directly at the building and then awoken to see Pete staring at him. The environment, the people's voices, the ache in his neck, when he awoke this morning, and the petrol fumes of the cars on the way here had all seemed like an ill-defined nightmare. Now that John understood it better, though not precisely, he knew the darkness was stronger when the truth of the building was concealed, which meant that Pete, effectively, was doing its bidding. If it couldn't erase John completely from this world, then it would at the very least discredit him.

Pete would scupper his chances of convincing the world of the truth about the building, because Pete was seen as equally important to the building's design. John's problems would continue, and there would be nothing he could do about it – not even legally, with his authority as Senior Partner in the firm, after having announced Pete as joint architect. Pete had obviously confirmed this with Zenith before John got here, because they had all already decided on the course of action, and John wouldn't be able to convince them otherwise. Pete would want to redeem his prestige and importance as joint architect of the building, regardless of the truth. John tried to think of a way to do this interview another day so that he could at least have twenty-four hours to consider. He glanced at Pete who was smiling contentedly.

'But do we have enough time to prepare?' John said.

'I feel it's best, with a situation like this, to strike as early as possible before it gets beyond our control,' Stacey said.

'We need to act quickly and decisively. The Muslims and the media are having a field day, and Zenith shares are dropping. Need I say more? Besides, we've got all day to prepare.'

Stacey wasn't afraid to show a little aggressive hostility in her tone towards John for having made such a mistake on television; but surely, as PR Officer, she should be thanking John and others like him for providing the situations that brought about the requirement for her job?

'Rachael Haas is a sympathetic interviewer', Stacey continued, 'and is trusted by the public. Have you heard her?'

John had heard her occasionally on the radio, this side of the amnesia, and nodded.

'Mr Wilkinson will be at the interview too, of course,' Stacey said. 'So, before we get down to the tactical preparation, are we all agreed as to the strategy?'

Wilkinson glanced at John with his deeply penetrating blue eyes. John, in turn, looked at Pete who was still smiling contentedly. Pete had agreed on the phone that he wouldn't concede anything until John was present. John must have really angered him on television for him to be behaving in such a way. John could ask to talk to him privately, but he felt a great pressure to comply immediately, and there would be nothing John could do to change their minds, anyway.

'I think so, yes,' John said, not knowing what else to do.

'Good,' Wilkinson said, slapping his small knees gently and standing up. 'I will inform the minister of our plan. And hopefully, calm him down a bit.' He walked to his large desk on the other side of the room and picked up the phone.

John remembered how the government had saved Zenith from bankruptcy. So to the public, it appeared complicit in the company's image.

'I'll inform the shareholders,' Mann said.

After mock question and answer sessions, they stopped for lunch, and John decided to nip home before further preparations and the interview this evening. He needed his own space.

He sat at the kitchen table and worried. If he were to refuse the interview, then Pete would still do it, ostensibly for the good of the company but, really, to enhance his own contribution to the design and, thus, diminish John's, so John had to do it.

The phone rang on the stand next to the sitting room door: 'Hello?'

'Hello, John,' a soft and velvety voice said.

John recognised the voice instantly, despite not having spoken to her for years.

'I wanted to talk to you,' she said.

'Okay.'

'About getting a divorce.'

John welcomed the surprise of hearing his wife's voice and her decision, finally, to get a divorce as a distraction from the Zenith problem tonight: 'I'll have to stop giving you the money, then.'

'Our money, John. I have as much right to that money as you.'

'So you're expecting half my money in the agreement?'

'No, John, not the money you've earned recently from the Zenith building. Congratulations on that, by the way.'

He already knew she hadn't talked to him during the amnesiac period, because there had been no divorce, or change in the money situation, and no major problems with their daughter that warranted a chat. At least, this was as far as he knew from his paper records and the card he had received from Gemma when he returned from hospital six months ago.

'Thank you.'

'I saw you on television last night. What was it you said about designing the building? You were only able to design it because you felt free for the first time in your life? And that that freedom came from the terrorist attack on the old building? Are you turning Muslim or something?'

'No, no. That's not what I meant.'

'Freedom, John!' she said abruptly. 'You dare to talk about freedom as if you had had a lack of it until then? In your twenties, you were lucky enough to have an inheritance from your parents to set up your own company. You were lucky enough to find me, too, and have a beautiful daughter. You were lucky enough to find a talented marketing man, like Pete, who would go into partnership with you. You achieved everything anybody could possibly want to achieve – a successful company, a loving family and lots of money. But, apparently, you didn't feel freedom until the terrorist attack! You don't have the right to talk about freedom.'

John tried to reflect on what she was saying with the phone sufficiently away from his ear. It was true. He had had all the freedom that a person could ask for and, although he didn't have the right to say that he didn't feel free for much of his life, it was still, nevertheless, true.

'What about you?' he said. 'You didn't feel free. Otherwise, you wouldn't have left me.'

'That was your fault. You suffocated both me and your daughter. I had to get out of there, and I had to take her with me, too.'

John remembered Gemma's wide grin and fearless eyes that blinked when she laughed. He felt the pain of not having seen her for so long: 'Where is she? Is she okay? Does she want to see me?'

There was a pause: 'I think so. Sometime, when she feels she wants to.'

Hillary's voice had calmed down and become more sympathetic, but John always believed she had brainwashed Gemma into not liking him: 'What's she doing?'

'She's in Africa, working hard. Anyway, I'll send you the divorce forms and see you in a couple months when I'm next in the country. Okay?'

'Sure.'

The call ended. The house appeared darker than before. He walked upstairs and trod warily to Gemma's old room. It was dark now, but he remembered the daylight hue when she used to run around and play with her toys. When she was older, she would gossip on the bed with her mother or with friends and boyfriends on the telephone. Where in Africa was she? What was she doing? What did she look like? And what had John done to make them want to leave him? He felt the loss of them, but the sadness couldn't manifest itself properly, and a strange, though not unfamiliar, stiffness spread through his insides like the freezing of lakes in winter.

13

Something dark and distorted crept through the environment, like vines or ivy growing through the cracks of walls. It was in the woods, the churned farmers' fields, the petrol station and, finally, the oncoming city as John drove back to the Zenith offices. It was everywhere and, yet, nowhere – too deep and essential to actually pinpoint or name.

When he returned to Wilkinson's office, ready to go over the preparations for a couple of hours before going to the radio station, he had decided he needed to consolidate the truth of his building to the world in absolute terms – without the interference of Pete. His plan was to subtly demean Pete's contribution to the design.

'Is something wrong?' Pete said as they went into the toilets together, just minutes before they were to leave for the radio station.

In a soft tone of voice, John said: 'Earlier, before I got to the office, you told me that we would first agree on something before Zenith pressurised us into doing anything. But when I arrived, you had already agreed the plan with Zenith which contributed to the pressure on me having to agree in the moment.'

'I couldn't see any other option. There *is* no other option.

It was useless for us to go and talk about it separately. It would have seemed like an insult to them.'

'Or perhaps, you like what the plan does for your reputation – reinvigorating your status as joint architect?'

'I really think this is the best move for Gowan Partnerships.'

'What about the truth of my building?'

The sound of Pete's piss hitting the enamel urinal became louder and then died away. Both men washed their hands in silence before walking out.

Everybody collected their things and began their journey to the radio station in the centre of town. In Princegate shopping centre, they took the escalators to the fourth floor, close to the ceiling's octagon-shaped skylights, where Blanworth Radio 101.6 was located. They stepped into a bright room with food machines and a coffee table. A young woman greeted them, and John, Wilkinson and Pete were then directed into another room, leaving Mann, Stacey and two bodyguards behind.

Inside the darker booth, the radio guests were greeted by the interviewer Rachael Haas – an overweight lady in her mid-forties with a crooked set of teeth, curly brown hair, a white blouse and a gold locket around her neck. She welcomed them cordially: 'Please take a seat. We should be ready in about five minutes.'

The quality of her voice – instantly recognisable from the radio voice to which they were all accustomed – was deliberate and direct.

They sat around a pale plastic, rectangular table with

Rachael at the head, Wilkinson and Pete on one side and John on the other. In the middle of the table were microphones with coloured muffs and wires trailing from them off the end of the table onto the floor. Each person had headphones. On one wall was a Blanworth Radio poster, written in red and blue, and on another was a large window that revealed another room with radio operatives wearing headphones.

After the preliminary introductions between Rachael and her guests, and the end of a music programme that had been conducted in another booth, the interview began: 'Now, many people in Blanworth and, for that matter, the rest of the country were shocked by yesterday's edition of Newsbeat on Channel 2 when John Gowan, architect of the new Zenith building—'

'*Joint* architect,' Pete said, butting in.

Rachael looked up and smiled an apology: 'Oh, I'm sorry, listeners. That was Pete Williams, the other architect of the building and somebody who you may remember being interviewed on this programme before, though not by me. He's giving me a friendly smile, so I don't think I offended him! But as I was going to say, many people were shocked when John Gowan, joint architect of the new Zenith building, stated that the building's design was creatively inspired by the terrorist attack on the old building. Here is a part of the recording from last night, beginning with Mr Gowan who's in conversation with Mr Wilkinson, the owner of Zenith Star Holdings, and Dianne Fielding, the interviewer:'

'Many people see the design qualities of the building as an

expression of the free society in which we live, but the great irony of the building – a building which many people see as a defence and glorification of our free society – is that it was creatively inspired *by* the attack on our freedom!'

'Are you advocating terrorism?' Fielding asked.

'No! I'm just telling you the inspiration behind the building's design.'

'But you mean that the sheer horror of the attack inspired your design?' Wilkinson asked.

'No, not the horror of the attack but the freedom *from* the attack!'

'But what do you mean by that?' Wilkinson asked.

'I mean, the way I felt as a result of the attack and the way Blanworth appeared to me as a result of the attack. There was danger in the air, excitement, shock and, indeed, horror, but it was all free. For the first time in life, I felt free. Everything was suddenly natural and loose. Something real had happened, away from the contrivances of normal living. And with this freedom available to me, I designed the building.'

'So, Mr Gowan, could you further elaborate on what you meant when you said that you felt inspired by the terrorist attack, and how that influenced the design of the building?'

'First of all, I would like to apologise to Mr Wilkinson and his company for any embarrassment I may have caused. It certainly wasn't my intention to embarrass them. I was suffering from nerves from being on television for the first time and, believe me, I was surprised, just as much as the listeners, when I said what I said in such a way – not to say that I disagree with it now but that I didn't explain myself properly.'

'Well, now you have the chance,' Rachael said.

'I'd like to make it clear that I don't have any real resentment towards the society in which I've lived all my life – not enough to warrant an attack on it! I appreciate all the freedoms we enjoy, and I'm certainly not a fundamentalist Muslim. However, I did feel good from the terrorist attack. Something real had happened – away from the normal state of life we seem to cherish – and people were genuinely shocked. This good feeling later produced a profound state of freedom in me. And with that, I went on to design the new building.'

'"Something real had happened,"' she said, repeating John's words. 'Do you feel life doesn't usually feel real?'

'That's right,' John said as he thought about his long, lonely days in his house, his boring days at the office designing uninteresting buildings, and his strange, detached days long ago when his wife and daughter lived with him. 'Life usually seems drab. Don't you feel that? Don't other people feel that?'

Before she could have time to answer, he continued speaking: 'I'm sure *you* don't – not with *your* job, your family if you have one, and the news that happens day after day in society. But that's not what I mean. Don't you feel it's all somehow pointless? Meaningless?'

She stared at him a moment and raised her eyebrows: 'And you felt life had meaning when Blanworth was attacked?'

'Yes! As I said, something *real* had happened. The obliteration, the commotion, the—'

'Death?'

'The freedom,' John said, remembering the day when he walked up to the site for the first time to view the damage. 'The freedom from the so-called freedom we're supposed to be living.'

'But what about those people who died?' she said, ignoring his last sentence. 'Did you not feel for them and their loved ones in the aftermath of the explosion – whilst you were feeling "free"?'

He shook his head, not wanting to be drawn into the idea of death being a part of the reason he had felt free. Otherwise, nobody would sympathise with what he was trying to say. 'Don't get me wrong, I felt sorry for those people and their families. Of course I didn't want anybody to die, but I didn't know any of them individually, so I wasn't personally affected.'

There was a brief moment of silence around the table, and John felt he had said something wrong – something strange – and he imagined the same kind of silence from many of the people listening to him in their homes.

'Anyway,' he said, 'people kept saying that we needed to defend our freedom in the aftermath of the explosion, but what freedom were they talking about? The life we usually lead! Do you really think my building was designed to celebrate that?'

He smirked, unable to suppress his sombre amusement.

Rachael looked at John thoughtfully: 'But perhaps, when people say "freedom", they mean the right to live the way they want to live – as long as it doesn't harm others – in a democratic and prosperous society.'

'But the freedom everybody is talking about runs insidiously deeper than that, Rachael,' John said, speaking from the depths of his being. 'We believe we are free and that, with this freedom, there is nothing more to life – nothing more to aspire to. We open ourselves up to a void that is prey to capitalism – competition and pointless success.'

'So you have political reasons for why you felt good from attack?'

'No, I don't! I'm not saying I'm for or against capitalism. What I'm saying is, freedom has become the new religion. With freedom in society as our only guiding light, we take it to mean freedom within our lives, too. And with that, we're denying ourselves the deeper aspects of what it means to be human.'

John paused, remembering what Janice had said of him during the amnesiac period – of him appearing free and unaffected by anything in life. And he remembered the moments before he crashed his car – the intense fast road and the dark countryside that engulfed it. This was the time he was becoming free. But, three and a half years later, he had lost it:

'On the night before construction began at the building site, I read a newspaper article entitled "The Freedom Building". The article praised the design of the building: a design that it said reflected the "freedom of society". The design of the building, however, had been inspired by the attack on society – when its "freedom" had been briefly obliterated. I realised how the irony of the article represented the truth of society, and I saw what the building would become. As a result, I fainted and hit my head.'

'You said you tripped at the time.'

'Yes, but now I conclude that I must have fainted, considering the way I was feeling at the time.'

Of course, John could not remember anything from that night, but fainting was the best rational explanation. The darkness had capitalised on his vulnerability created by his realisation and stolen his true self.

'When I woke up, I no longer felt I had the creativity, the drive, the ambition to continue the project of the building, which was why I let my business partner, Pete, commence duties at the site. My building is a hypocrisy, a symbol of our freedom in society, and it will continue to be a hypocrisy until we understand its design was inspired by an attack on the so-called freedom of this society. That is what I'm trying to explain here today.'

Wilkinson lowered his faint eyebrows slightly, showing his dislike for John's words but, so far, the things John had said had been sanctioned earlier by Stacey, the PR woman. Rachael stared at him a moment, calculating how to respond: 'But what of others who say its appearance is representative of a free society in the sense that it is complicated in its make-up, perhaps as in the diversity of peoples and in the complications of finance and capitalism, but its overall appearance is simple, allowing for the existence of this complicated make-up which is free?'

John had heard this description of the building before: a description which didn't literally betray the appearance of the building. Therefore, it was one that he could hear: 'I don't doubt that when people see my building they see freedom. They call it "the freedom of this society", but that cannot be attributed to my building, because the freedom I experienced – that which inspired me to produce such a design – was instigated by an attack on the freedom of this society!'

'So you were lying, at the beginning of the television interview, when you said that the freedoms we enjoy in this society were the inspiration behind the building?'

'I knew how many people I would offend if I were to tell the truth, including the families and friends of those who died. But, later in the interview, I couldn't hold back the truth any longer, aided by the fact I was nervous and speaking without a controlled mind.'

'But, of course, Mr Gowan is not the only architect,' Wilkinson said. 'Pete Williams jointly designed the building, so what does he think?'

Pete opened his mouth to answer but Rachael interjected: 'Before we get to Mr Williams, I would like to discuss the significance of Mr Gowan's remarks for the Zenith company. Mr Wilkinson,' she said, turning to him, 'Zenith shares have dropped considerably since the television interview, and so it is in your financial interest to rectify the problem created by Mr Gowan on television. What exactly is the problem, do you think?'

'Good evening. Let me first of all accept Mr Gowan's apology publicly. I know that he didn't mean to cause Zenith any trouble.'

'Thank you,' John said.

'The problem was, simply, that Mr Gowan didn't explain himself fully on television, because he left it too late in the show. Of course, I was surprised by what he said, because he hadn't told me before the interview that he was going to say what he did, but he didn't intend to attack Zenith policy at all.'

'But what was the lack of understanding, do you think, that caused people to sell Zenith shares?'

'Mr Gowan said what he said towards the end of a heated debate between myself and Abdul Hassim, and some people interpreted his words as siding with Abdul Hassim when, really, he did nothing of the sort. He did not side with Abdul, and he did not side with me, either.'

'But do you acknowledge that the design of the Zenith building was not inspired by our free society but by an attack on our free society?'

'If it was designed by a person who believes that he couldn't have designed it without the inspiration gained from a terrorist attack, then we must take him at his word. But, of course, there was more than just one person who designed the building. Mr Williams the joint designer of the building is sitting with us.'

Rachael lifted her eyebrows and looked at Pete: 'But what role in designing the building did you have, Mr Williams, if Mr Gowan designed the building from the inspiration he received from the terrorist attack?'

Pete smiled and adjusted his glasses: 'Well, first let me say, I actually believe in the free society in which we live. I know there are problems of course, as there are in any society, but that doesn't mean I should feel excited by an attack that killed hundreds of innocent people. The terrorist attack, I found repulsive and disgusting.'

'You seem quite angry at your partner's words.' Rachael said.

'Well, in a way, I am. My inspiration behind the design was the need to give hope back to Blanworth. We'd suffered a terrible attack – something which nobody in Blanworth was ready for – and we all needed something to look to as a beacon of hope for mankind: something which would not only show terrorists that we're not afraid of their actions and threats, but something which reflected the beauty of our way of life.'

'And was this what you were thinking when you helped to design the building?'

'You say "helped", and it's true John was the first to begin designing the building on his own at home – I've said that many times before in previous interviews – but after he showed the design to me at the office, I decided to design something completely different.'

Pete's face, his glasses, his square jawline and his colourful tie suddenly seemed to change from an ostentatious, extravagant, ugly, but familiar appearance to something subversive, strange, inhuman and evil. John's jaw dropped. What was Pete saying? There had been no plans in the preparations for the interview earlier to say such a thing. In fact, John had secretly hoped to demean Pete's declared contribution to the design of the building: it would have come naturally after John explaining he had designed the building from the inspiration of the terrorist attack and then showed the plans to Pete. But, now, Pete was saying that he, Pete Williams, designed it!

Rachael's tongue darted mischievously out of her mouth: 'Do you mean the building being constructed now is your design?'

'Yes,' Pete said, 'totally. I couldn't possibly do anything with John's initial design. It lacked warmth. It lacked substance. When I looked at it, I thought this is not what Blanworth needs. I don't doubt John is telling the truth about his initial inspiration, which is probably why his design appeared ugly. To give him credit, some people may have liked it in its own strange way. But I ask you, Rachael, can you really look at the beautiful design of the building that we have today and believe that its inspiration came from the horror of the terrorist attack? Isn't it more likely that it came from the beautiful freedoms that we all enjoy?'

Rachael smiled, clearly happy with the conflict Pete was creating with John – live on radio: 'But why would you be saying all this now?'

John nodded with the question whilst desperately trying to think what he could say to discredit Pete.

'Well, my intention is not to discredit John in any way,' Pete said. 'Let me make that point clear. Not at all. He's a good architect. However, after listening to him speaking yesterday on television, then again here on the radio, and with so many people looking to the Zenith building as a beacon of hope, I feel I have to transcend my loyalty to the senior partner of my firm and say something. It's my design that people see today, not his.'

'Mr Gowan?' Rachael said.

They all looked at John, and he desperately needed to say something to overcome his shock. Wilkinson looked at him with deeply threatening blue eyes as if daring him to object. Had Pete and Zenith hoodwinked John earlier and planned to attack him on the radio – just as John had planned to attack Pete? If so, wouldn't Wilkinson have known that John would defend himself?

'I have to say, Pete,' John said, 'you're not speaking the truth.'

'Oh, really?' Pete said.

'The initial design that I produced is basically what you see today. There's no change. And if listeners were to think about everything I've already said, they would realise that I haven't even needed you to design this building, because it was me that came up with its initial conception. Sure, you did do some dogmatic, consequential work later with internal layout and other non-aesthetic considerations, but the image of the building – the way we see it today in its design – is the way I conceived it in the beginning.'

Rachael's tongue darted outside her mouth again: 'Are you saying that Mr Williams shouldn't even deserve to be known as joint architect?'

'I haven't liked to say it. But, yes.'

'Then why did you name him joint architect?'

'Because it strengthened the firm's image and our professional relationship at the time. However, now that Pete is saying that he was the one who designed the building, I feel I have to speak the truth, because I feel strongly about the integrity of the building.'

'There seems to be a major difference of opinion,' Rachael said gleefully, 'which suggests that somebody has to be lying. Do you have the designs you initially produced to see whether they are anything like the designs now?'

John guessed the originals were probably amongst the designs he couldn't see in his house, but to try to show them in his present condition and know which ones they were, as opposed to later adjustments according to Zenith requirements, would be impossible: 'No, only up-to-date, relevant ones.'

'You destroyed your originals?' Pete asked sarcastically.

John ignored his question: 'But if you designed the building, Pete, then why haven't you spoken out before? Why didn't you say something when I told the world, falsely, that you jointly designed the building – or even before then?'

Pete appeared calm and frank, channelling his focus on John: 'Well, it's an unofficial title so there didn't seem to be any point. I don't think you had explicitly said you were the sole architect before that point, anyway. So I didn't feel aggrieved. You were the senior partner of the firm, and the press naturally looked to you as the architect. Ironically, once you did acknowledge me, I did feel upset, because it was really my design, but I consoled myself with the knowledge that I probably wouldn't even have tried to design the building without your initial enthusiasm, so I didn't mind too much.'

John still couldn't believe what he was hearing: how Pete was going against him in such a way. They must have planned this attack when John was away from the Zenith offices today. They would have known he would never have gone along with it, so they pretended to have another plan, just to get him into the radio station.

John turned on Wilkinson, fearless: 'Who do you believe designed the building, Mr Wilkinson?'

Wilkinson held up his hands: 'I couldn't possibly comment. It has nothing to do with me.'

'But I'm sure you must have an opinion. Didn't you liaise with us before construction began?'

'I and some of my employees dealt with both you and Mr Williams at that time, going over details of the building and looking later for contractors and sub-contractors. I couldn't possibly give an opinion, though, as to who designed the building. All I know is that Pete has been working at the site as the resident architect since construction began.'

'But surely, Mr Wilkinson, you hope listeners will believe that Pete designed the building? He's saying that he designed it with the inspiration of our free society, which is the way you have promoted the design of the building.'

'Frankly, I'm confused at the moment. I'm not exactly sure what's happened in this interview. We came here so that you could both explain yourselves more fully about your shared inspiration behind the building, but now each of you is saying that you solely designed the building.'

'But who do you believe?' said John.

'I told you, I have no idea. It's an issue between you.'

John stared into his deep blue eyes.

'But may I ask, Mr Wilkinson,' Rachael said, 'was it not a strategy of yours to bring Mr Williams to this interview to say that he designed the building to counter Mr Gowan's comments?'

'To remind listeners that there is another architect of the Zenith building, yes. I don't deny the fact that Mr Gowan's comments on television temporarily harmed Zenith, so I wanted to remind the world that there is another architect and that his inspiration came, not from the terrorist attack but, from the society in which we live. Mr Gowan was aware that I wanted this to be said in a radio interview, and he agreed to it. This is why Mr Williams is here with us now. However, the argument over who solely designed the building is totally unexpected.'

Rachael's eyes were wide open, clearly loving the drama. Now everybody in the world would be deciding whether

John or Pete designed the building, and John feared that Pete was the victor, because Pete had been the first to say he was the sole architect. Those that hated Zenith, though, would side with John, but all the rest, including the politically indifferent, would side with Pete. After all, who would want to believe the harsh truth of where the inspiration for the building's design really came from when the alternative was far more comforting? John looked at Pete who was staring down at the table, as if hurt and wounded by John's comments.

John needed to leave. Zenith and Pete had betrayed him. Wilkinson was far too calculating a man and Pete far too socially manipulative for Pete's claims, that he solely designed the building, not to have been planned.

'I apologise for arguing here today,' John said, trying to sound reasonable, 'but I cannot sit here any longer and listen to these men or, at least, Pete Williams say I didn't design the building.'

John feared public repercussions causing further embarrassment for Zenith and added: 'Despite the argument with my partner just now, though, I hope I've come here and said what I needed to say and will not have tarnished Zenith's reputation last night on television in any way.'

With that, he pulled off the headphones, looked at Pete, whose head was still lowered towards the table, neglected to look at Wilkinson and walked out the door.

As he descended to the shopping levels, John felt numb from what had happened. Far from successfully claiming that he alone had designed the Zenith building, it was Pete who had said it first, so John's reaction probably seemed like a retaliatory defence rather than the truth. Or, perhaps, Zenith's plan to hijack John with the use of Pete was obvious to the audience.

Pete had now become the embodiment of his problems. He stood in direct conflict with John's need to convince the world of the truth of the building. The ill-defined problems of society, of people, of the world and of everything which had made John feel uneasy, throughout his life, now had a name. The darkness was Pete, and he and Zenith had to be overcome.

'Gowan!' A voice cried, high above.

John looked up through the large gap, to the level just below the ceiling's octagon-shaped skylights, and saw Mann looking down at him, his handlebar moustache unmistakable, even from that distance. Pete appeared behind him, looking down.

'Wait, John,' Pete shouted.

John felt tempted to walk away, but he wanted to hear what Pete had to say. Without Mann, Pete appeared at the bottom of the escalator a minute later and approached John. He seemed both sad and terrified behind his thick black-rimmed glasses.

'I'm sorry, John. I'm sorry.' He stopped and stood still.

'I know why you did it,' John said.

'It was for us, for the company. Zenith were scared when you went off home for lunch this afternoon. They thought the plan of me simply reminding listeners that there was another architect of the Zenith building wouldn't overcome the damage you caused to them last night. That's why I agreed to this plan. I knew you wouldn't agree to it, but I felt I had to – for us, for the company, for securing contracts in the future. Otherwise, nobody would want to hire us, no matter how talented we were. We couldn't afford to have a firm like Zenith with government backing against us. Who knows what they could do!'

'Legally, they couldn't have done a thing against us. I said what I thought was the truth about my own building on television and, whilst it did have detrimental effects on their business, they couldn't have sued us for slander.'

Pete scratched his neatly-combed hair erratically: 'Well, they had me pinned up against the wall at the time, what with the government backing them, and everybody desperately wanting to clear up the mess you'd caused on television. I still believe I did the right thing.'

'But I argued against you. I said you weren't the architect but that I was.'

'We guessed you would, and Zenith were fine with that scenario. People wouldn't know who to believe, and that would still be a better situation for them than me simply saying I was joint architect. Anyway, we have to wait to see the public's and the shareholders' response.'

John didn't trust Pete's motivations, because he believed Pete's ego would have gleefully seized the chance of claiming he was sole architect: 'But some people will think you solely designed the building, Pete. Don't you think that's a terrible thing?'

Pete just stared at John a moment, not saying anything – as if he truly believed he designed the building. Finally, he said: 'People will believe what they want to believe. If they disagree with how Zenith conducts its business overseas, then they'll believe you designed the building. And if they like Zenith, they'll believe I designed it. It's political, so who cares!'

Pete was speaking the truth in this regard; it was political. Whoever was believed to be the real architect, the legacy of the building would be shrouded in political agenda: either pro Pete because people believed in the defence of a free society, or pro John because they were against Zenith and its international dealings. The truth of his building, of its actual free birth, would be lost forever.

'You know, I could now say that Zenith put you up to it and that you've admitted it to me,' John said wearily.

'We both know Zenith and I would deny that, and I would be forced to gather support that I designed the building from our employees – for the good of the company, you understand.'

John found it hard to battle against the darkness and feared the future of always being bound to the hypocrisy of the building, never finding the freedom he had had during the amnesiac period.

Later that day, John spoke to Mann, in person, who apologised for the way things had transpired but stopped short of admitting Zenith's involvement. Mann did admit he was happy, though, as if to say: don't worry anymore about the television interview, but don't try attacking us for what we did as a result.

The next day at the office, John could sense that everybody except Janice believed Pete was the true designer and that Pete undoubtedly enjoyed the prestige. Outside the building, the two men greeted reporters – one of whom worked for the Blanworth Express, the other for a national newspaper – and gave a statement saying the argument was now internal and that they wouldn't be answering anymore questions from the media.

Over the next few days, there were political arguments about the legacy of the building in the News, but most of the newspapers were saying it was still a symbol of a free country because, in addition to Pete claiming he designed it and the political support from the government, the public's appetite for it was so strong.

John's blindness to the building remained, weighing him down and crippling his life. The environment grew weird and perplexing and as the darkness delved deeper into his brain, he no longer saw an enemy and something to fight against but, instead, an apathy for all things. Life was sometimes lifeless or, at other times, utterly petrifying for no apparent reason – or a mixture of both. He searched for reality in the urban landscape, touching the stones of buildings, trying to ascertain how they were constructed, but even the cathedral, a place of grandeur and retreat in the past, couldn't give him what he was looking for.

The lack of reality did not confine itself to inanimate objects. People were becoming shadowy figures within this environment, too. John couldn't get a sense of their lives, their ability to live. Those in the office looked to Pete with the uttermost respect and belief, but his kaleidoscopic image emanated a rich tapestry of darkness for John. Janice was the only one left who believed in him, or so it seemed, but his growing detachment from reality meant he wasn't capable of wanting to be with her, or needing to ask for her help. Her advancements for intimacy were no longer appreciated; and soon, the close relationship that had been established during the amnesiac period was gone.

14

On a rare day that he was feeling more normal and able to cope with people, John went into work to get away from his house and his thoughts and to familiarise himself with the office. He did this every couple of weeks or so. Janice greeted him, sitting at her desk as usual in front of his private office.

'Pete still wants to speak to you.'

'Since when?' he asked.

'Don't you remember? I rang you last week and told you he wanted to talk to you. He tried to phone you, himself, but you didn't answer.'

'Is he in?'

'Yep.'

John noticed she appeared sad and wondered whether she was still having problems with her divorce. He walked over to Pete's office and went in. Pete was on the other side of the curvaceous table, wearing a red bow tie today with both ends tucked bizarrely into his shirt. Behind him was the backdrop of houses rising on Toxon's hills.

'Listen, John,' he said, putting down the phone, 'you know that I'm very sorry for what happened on radio nine months ago – for what I did. But you also know that I was forced into that position by Zenith. If I hadn't done what I did, they would probably have cancelled the radio interview and attacked us in some other underhand way, in an attempt to re-establish their integrity.'

'Sure,' John said dismissively, sitting back into the leather chair.

'We've known each other for a long time, haven't we?'

John shrugged.

Pete smiled good-naturedly: 'In college you were a year above me, and I barely knew you. It was only after college, when we bumped into each other in Blanworth, that we learnt we grew up in the same city. A few days later, you told me you had money from your inheritance and were looking for a junior partner to form a new company. And I think we've now achieved more than we ever dreamed of.'

Pete touched his side parting carefully and adjusted his black-rimmed glasses: 'Have you spoken to any of our employees today?'

'Janice – who said you wanted to speak to me.'

'Did she say anything?'

'No.'

'Nobody else?'

John shook his head.

'Well, I asked nobody to tell you.'

Pete sat silently a moment. Then suddenly, he straightened his back as if finding courage for what he was about to say: 'If you had talked to any of them, you might have discovered that all except Janice – who's never been PA to both of us, anyway, and whom I didn't even bother asking until yesterday because I knew it would be futile – have decided to work for me in a new company that I will be forming after the Zenith project is complete.'

'What!'

'Williams Enterprise, it will be called. And the dissolution of Gowan Partnerships will be totally legal, in adherence to our contract. I'm giving you enough notice, and so will our employees.'

John let Pete's words settle uncomfortably inside his brain. The firm that he had set up with his parent's inheritance – when both had died of cancer and wanted him to do something meaningful with it – the firm that he had spent his professional life building, the firm that had given him the opportunity to raise a family and build his own home was now being destroyed by his junior partner.

'Why?' John said.

'Without you and with a new company name, I will be able to secure better contracts.'

'How?'

'The latest example – Cramer & Sons. You remember I wanted us to design their new office building, once we finished the Zenith contract?'

John remembered Pete mentioning something about the firm Cramer & Sons last month.

'Well,' Pete said, 'I got in touch with them, but they were not interested, John – like other companies. They said it was because of your behaviour with Zenith on television and our consequential political involvement with Zenith that makes them not want to be associated with us. I talked to the CEO on the phone. He spoke candidly about not wanting to be associated with an architectural firm that had become politicised. He said we got too involved with Zenith's problems, and he didn't want that association. He said it was specifically you whom he didn't want to be associated with. Therefore, I began to think of forming a new company without you. Why should both of us be affected?'

John was feeling far more alert now. The reality of the environment, including Pete's curvaceous desk and the red-bricked houses on the hill through the window, no longer appeared smudged and lifeless but dark, distorted and intimidating with Pete sitting in the middle.

'But you're the one associated with politics,' John said. 'You defended the building as a symbol of this country's freedom, allying yourself with Zenith and its business practises, albeit indirectly.'

'Yes, but you were the one who started the controversy. What I did was nothing as bad as you did, which was to claim the design was indebted to the attack on this country's freedom.'

'But I designed the Zenith building, Pete – not you.'

Pete sighed: 'Shall we stop the farce, John? Just for one moment, shall we speak the truth in private? I designed the building, John – not you. The only reason I went along with you was because you were the senior partner, and I could do nothing about it – not until you cocked-up on television and I had help from Zenith.'

John couldn't believe what he was hearing, even from Pete: 'It's finally gone to your head – this image of grandeur – has it?'

Pete grinned: 'Fine.'

Pete's wide grin, his perfect white teeth and his black-rimmed glasses suddenly began to pain John's eyes. The walls in the room seemed to move towards John, and he felt a pain beginning to emanate from his forehead, exactly where he had it when he woke up in hospital: 'Are you the enemy that's been against me all my life, stopping me from fulfilling my potential but stealing its results when I finally did produce something worthy?'

Pete looked at him incredulously: 'Since I've known you, you've always needed to design a great building. I've never got in your way. When the opportunity finally came, you failed, and it was me that created a great design. You never came to terms with it, and I think this inability to face the truth created problems for you – genuine delusionary problems which began on the night you hit your head at the site, probably intentionally.'

The pain grew worse and so did the malevolent nature of the room. None of what Pete was saying was the truth. He was always the egomaniac, and now he believed his own lies. He had always been part of the problem ever since John went into business with him. Pete was the man who was fake and unreal, the man who played politics – much of what John disliked about the world. It was for this reason John went into business with him: he was so good at promoting the firm and gaining contracts with clients.

John staggered to his feet. Darkness and twisted reality encircled Pete's being like the surrounding space of a black hole. Mesmerised by the horror, John stared a moment, far enough away to observe the spectacle without falling into its evil, before turning quickly and leaving the room. A couple of employees glanced at him with demonic expressions as he tried to focus on the exit. In the lift, the mirrored walls showed a strange, shadowy reflection, ruffled and bent, and John closed his eyes, trying not to be sick. The foyer's sliding doors opened too slowly, and he stumbled into the fresh air, reaching for a cigarette before proceeding towards the shopping centre with the intention of going to his car.

Green fields flashed by. Distant bulbous cooling towers belched white steam into the sunny air as cows stood in groups, chewing the cud. After turning onto the road that led directly to his house and driving a couple of miles, he took his foot off the accelerator and let the car slow down, gliding over to the left to avoid a hooting car from the opposite direction. By the time he approached the bend he was going slowly enough not to use the brake. The car almost stopped halfway round, and he slumped his head onto the steering wheel, pushing it anticlockwise and turning the car into the ditch – where he crashed. In the silence that ensued, his stomach muscles contracted intermittently, but no tears escaped his eyes.

With his head slumped on the kitchen table, John mumbled to himself: 'January 25th . Male suicide is high this time of year. Autumn goes quickly with the anticipation of Christmas and New Year. Then, in a flash, it's gone. Reality hits on the first morning back at work. So for some, it's a trip to the medicine cabinet. That reminds me, sort out my Life Assurance today. Wonder how much money the NHS spends on counselling for failed attempts? Surprised the government hasn't introduced prescription discounts for this time of year to coincide with sales. Hillary liked shopping this time of year – gave her the excuse to get away from me. "A good buy, Hillary? Goodbye £400!" She spent an awful lot on dresses and birthday presents for second cousins. "But we haven't seen them in years," I would say. Money became my hollow passion – kept the blood from clotting. I remember the relief it gave her to argue, and perhaps I did it intentionally. Arguments certainly gave her the excuse she wanted. At first she looked for them elsewhere, accusing me of having an affair with Janice, but I denied that without much conviction, which she didn't seem to like. Anyway, an attempt to move Christmas Day to January 25th was the last straw – or the straw she was looking for. "Think of the money we'd save!" And seven years ago today, I came home to discover a note on the kitchen table. I found it difficult to react.'

There was a knock at the door. He raised his head from the cold pine kitchen table. Hillary had wanted to meet him today and had assured him, in her email, that it was a coincidence it was January 25th . But surely, she saw it as some kind of poetic justice? He didn't care. The anticipation of her presence, having not seen her for so many years, woke him partially from his apathy.

'John!' she shrieked from outside.

He opened the door. His wife stood there, looking almost the same as when he last saw her, with curly, brown hair below her shoulders, rounded cheeks that were a little thinner and glowing white teeth.

'Well, aren't you going to invite me in?' she said.

He gestured her in with his hand.

She stamped snow onto the mat, walked past him, stinking of pleasant perfume, and sat immediately at the table with her handbag in front of her: 'I like what you've done to the place – cobwebs, dirty dishes, the lack of heating.'

He rotated the thermostat dial on the wall: 'How did you get here?'

'George drove me.'

Through the window, a bearded man, wearing a chequered cap, was sat in a sports car.

'The reason for the divorce?'

'There are more reasons than him, John.'

'Tea?'

She stared at him a moment, then nodded.

'What about Romeo?'

'Are you jealous?'

John realised he might be and felt good for it: an increasing sense of life pumping through his veins. He put the kettle on.

'I regret what I said on the phone,' she said, lighter in tone.

'What do you mean?'

'I shouldn't have got angry.'

'I'm not sure I remember what you said.'

'I got angry at what you said on television – that you had never felt free in your life, not until the terrorist attack.'

John vaguely remembered talking about freedom, but it didn't concern him anymore: 'Oh, yes.'

The kettle clicked and he poured the teas.

'I think you were telling the truth about your not feeling free for much of your life, though.' she said. 'The overall reason I left you was because, to use your word, you didn't feel free. And it was damaging our daughter, too.'

He sat opposite her with the drinks: 'Well, I'm sorry about that.'

'But, even though you are to blame for breaking up our family,' she said, 'you are not to blame for harming yourself.'

John smirked: 'Thanks.'

'And from listening to you on the radio subsequently, it sounds like you've tried to understand the problem.'

John was remembering things properly now – the television interview, the radio interview and all his problems related to the building – truly awakening him from his apathetic slumber. The kitchen became a more fearful place as the darkness revealed itself to him again: 'Well, as you said, it's a lack of freedom that's always been the problem for me.'

'But what do you mean by it, and why did it destroy our marriage?'

John stared at her, the darkness, that had always been there, distorting her rounded cheeks and her perfume into something strange and depressing.

'Was it work? Was it the architectural world, the bureaucracy and red tape? Was it the way we lived as a family? What was it?'

John lit a cigarette and concentrated on the pleasure of addiction to help him overcome the odds: 'The answer begins with losing my freedom the night before construction of the Zenith building began. As you must have heard in the television interview, I fell that night and awoke in hospital. Since then, Pete has worked at the site, and I've not really done anything more on the building. I had problems, you see, problems that I tried to conceal because whenever I did come close to telling anybody about them, those problems would get worse, and I feared they might consume and take me away.'

'John, what are you talking about?'

'It doesn't matter now because I've lost everything – the building, my family, my business, my essence… There is no worse place I can go. Initially, I believed these problems were exclusive to the building, because they were all connected to not being able to see or understand it properly.'

'You can't see your building?'

He contemplated whether he should tell her. The reality of the room, though oppressive, remained constant. There was no threat of it taking him anywhere else. He didn't feel dizzy or about to faint.

'No. Whenever I look at it, I see a blur, and I have realised that the blindness to the building, with all the associated problems, has exposed a problem I have had all my life.'

'And what is that – the problem you have had all your life?' she asked, seemingly taking the blindness to his building for granted.

'The inability to feel, see or experience freedom – or, at least, what freedom means to me.'

'The problem you had when I was living with you?'

'Yes, I could not see freedom then, and I can't see it now. Only, then I was more ignorant of that fact. I felt trapped in a pointless and sometimes horrific existence – a reality from which I could not escape.'

'And your family couldn't help you in any way?'

John shrugged his shoulders: 'If I'd known exactly what I didn't have but felt, at least, I was on the path towards freedom, then I would have quite happily lived the family life. Indeed, I would have desired it. I would have loved myself, loved you and loved Gemma.'

'But you didn't?'

'No, but I found what I was looking for when Blanworth was attacked. The atrocity seemed to open a gateway to something deeper inside me, something that was more profound in life and something that overcame my general condition of dissatisfaction and mind decay. Perhaps, this is deeper inside us all.' He paused and sighed, remembering the moments before he crashed the car: how the road and the fast-approaching bend united to reveal an overwhelming surge of energy. 'I may be verging on the spiritual. I don't know, but I'm sure I found something more to life than what we know or think we have.'

'You sound more like the man I married, John.'

'What do you mean?'

Her large eyes relaxed, and she smiled: 'When I first met you, there was something inside you that you wanted to express or seek. And architecture seemed to be your means for doing it.'

John thought back to the early years and remembered being happy with his new business and new wife: 'That was something different. I was young then, with my whole life ahead of me. It was natural to be happy and express that in my designs.'

'No, that's not what I mean. Don't you remember that there was something more to architecture for you than just the superficial designs?'

He remembered Hillary, in the last years, trying to convince him that he'd changed from the person she'd married. He was tempted to stop listening, as he always used to do. But now, he felt she was kindling old memories inside him: 'What do you mean?'

'I look at the Zenith building now, and I think: You actually did it!'

John was excited by her memories of his younger self and that connection to the Zenith building: 'Can you explain a little more?'

'Wait a second.'

She walked out the front door, said something indistinctly to George and returned to hover above him with her large eyes: 'Where are your old things? Your old paintings and writings that you had when we first met. Have you touched them since I last saw you?'

He remembered the things she was talking about as being some pictures he'd painted and some poetry he'd written in his teenage years and early twenties: 'No, not that I remember. They're probably still in the basement. I've always meant to clear it out.'

'Yes, and I didn't let you – not after you burnt all your old architectural designs from college.'

John reflected a moment and remembered something he hadn't recalled in a very long time: how much pain his old architectural designs had given him. He'd achieved high marks for them in college but decided to burn them because they seemed to be too free, too painful. He was about thirty when he did that.

'Come on. I want to show you something,' she said.

He followed her from the kitchen into the dining room, which was located at the front of the house on the other side – completely dusty now, with a walnut table and ornament cabinets – and through a door, at the back of the room, which led to the basement. She switched on the light at the top of the stairs and stepped briskly into the depths. As he followed, the concrete steps were cold through John's socks, and the air was thick with age. She switched on another light at the bottom and walked past the wine racks to a large blue chest in the corner on the ground. John hadn't drunk the wine for a long time, content with the whisky upstairs in the drinks cabinet.

'You have the key on you?' she asked.

He walked to a wooden shelf that had bits of metal and wood strewn across it. He lifted an empty clay pot and saw the rusty key beneath. He walked back to the chest with his head lowered, so as not to scrape it on the ceiling, crouched down sideways to the chest, so his shadow wouldn't darken the lock, and clicked the old key into place. The lock opened, and he pushed the lid up and over so that it rested on the wall behind, with its golden hinges exposed.

'So, what do you want?' he said impatiently.

She crouched down and looked into the chest. Inside was a huge heap of notepads and drawings contained in cardboard wallets that were tied with string. She pushed her hand into the chest, foraged down a few inches and randomly pulled out a cardboard wallet. She turned to let the light shine on it and unravelled the string. Upon opening it, a painting fell out into her lap and then onto the ground. It was upside down from where John was crouched.

Despite its awkward angle on the floor and the many years since he had last seen it, John recognised it instantly. It was a painting he'd done of office buildings in Blanworth on one sunny summer afternoon when he was about sixteen. Light reflected off their windows, and people walked on the pavements. The buildings were erected in the sixties and still standing today, not far from the city centre. They were poorly constructed, built of grey and brown brick and seen by John today as hideous. But he remembered that day well:

how he sat opposite the buildings, uncaring of what passers-by might think, and painted the picture. He remembered finding them beautiful. How odd, he thought.

Hillary picked up the painting, smiled and gave it to him. The colours on the page were faint and delicate, yet they were expressive and evocative. He felt something as he looked at it, almost mesmerised now: how things seemed on that day in his youth, and how everything seemed perfect. A feeling, resonating deep within him, rose into his consciousness and burst like an air bubble on the water's surface.

'You may wonder why I wanted to come down here, John,' she said, placing her hand beneath his chin and raising his head to her eye level. She seemed very pretty in the bulb light, her eclectically coloured eyes glinting like the windows in the picture. She looked at his eyes, his nose, his mouth and glanced down at the painting: ' *This* is why.'

'Because I liked to paint once?'

'Because you *believed* in something.'

'In painting?

'You enjoyed painting, poetry and *especially* buildings, but it was all for an underlying reason. I never quite understood what you meant in our chats when I first met you, but you used to tell me things which seemed exotic – things that you saw. You wanted to *do* something: to replicate the things you *saw* in architecture. This, at least, was what you told me.'

John vaguely remembered the chats when he had told her how he wanted to design great and wonderful buildings. As he did so, he remembered how, in his youth, he would see occasional glimpses of a world that was far more real and elaborate than the normal world he was used to. At that time, these glimpses made him want that world and search for it. It was almost an unconscious searching which was only ever vocalised when he talked to Hillary. It almost sounded stupid to him when he spoke it aloud, but he felt he could tell her because she loved him, so it didn't matter how stupid it sounded. His reason for pursuing architecture was to somehow recreate this world through his designs.

He looked at the painting and glimpsed the experience of that world again. The environment glittered in radiance. He looked at his wife who seemed even more beautiful than moments ago – her eyelashes, her hair and her reason for being here in the cellar – and he felt the urge to touch her.

Spontaneously, he said: 'It was a different way of seeing things. And I wanted to replicate that world, which I occasionally glimpsed, in the design of buildings.'

She smiled.

He felt the words with the physical intensity that revelations can enable one to feel – mind and body uniting and trembling with energy. But suddenly, a blur started to overcome the exhilaration; and immediately, he began to feel deflated again: 'But something stops me from experiencing it.'

'What is it?' she said.

'A dark, heavy void. A few years into our marriage, it came from seemingly nowhere, insidiously affecting me and permeating my life. When we lived in Blanworth, I began to feel it there, so I decided to work in Toxon where, in the bricks and the roads, life seemed more real and free. That helped for a while. And when we had enough money from my business, I fled from our house in Blanworth to move to the countryside, thinking I would escape it for good. But, no matter where I went, it found me and ate into my life. With nowhere left to go, I didn't feel I could fight it because I didn't know what it was, and I plunged into darkness as my halcyon reality became a forgotten romance.'

'Do you know what it is now?'

'I can see it indirectly because it hides the building. When I grew older, and my inspiration for life became too elusive in a society that did not reflect my inspiration, I consequently denied myself higher ways of experiencing life. The days became claustrophobic, constricted and oppressive. And I know I changed beyond recognition.

'When Blanworth was attacked and a higher reality emerged, I designed a building from it. But then, society did what it does best, claiming my building, my freedom, even humanity's freedom, for itself. And the darkness returned to me.'

'Then, you just have to find a way of convincing people of the truth.'

'I can't. I've already tried.'

She rested her hand on top of his head: 'Don't give up. It's not even completed yet. Who knows what your building's legacy will be, even a year from now.'

There was a distant knock on the door from upstairs. She

looked at her watch and stood: 'Listen, I've got to go, but you can phone me anytime.'

John stood, holding the painting.

'So, do you have them?' she asked.

John walked out of the basement with the painting in his hand, through the dining room and into the kitchen. He collected the divorce papers from a chair underneath the kitchen table, and gave them to her. She kissed him on the cheek and left the house.

He stood at the door and watched the car drive through the snow, up to the front gate and away. He felt a bitterly cold breeze on his chest, and the pale blue and white sky made him feel utterly alone. It seemed strange but, with the car now gone, it suddenly felt as if the wife had never come and that what had happened was just a dream.

He bent down and crunched snow in his bare hand to feel more real. His fingers began to burn at the joints. He liked the feeling, surprisingly, and visualised flames emanating from them. Fire and destruction filled his imagination, and he remembered the destruction of the old building when he visited it for the first time – the rubble, the crowd, the firemen and policeman, the sunlight, the excitement ...

He looked up and saw the thin line of distant trees marking the boundary of his property. The loneliness of the environment seemed to be dispersing, as if it were beginning to reveal its true, friendly identity. The trees seemed to wave back at him as the breeze tickled their leaves. The pale blue and white sky offered a blanket of soothing coldness, and he smiled as he began to experience the world he always looked for.

But he knew it was only a glimmer. The trees had already begun to stop waving. The legacy of his new building would forever be a burden to his soul. In despair, he imagined pushing the shadowy image of his new building down into the ground with his hand and it shattering across Blanworth, just as the old building had done. A huge adrenaline rush of excitement overcame him, his heart pumping like a fist into the back of his chest. He liked the feeling so much that he imagined planning an operation, just like the terrorists, to destroy the building. His heart beat harder and faster.

15

A couple of months later, on the day of the Opening Ceremony, John said goodbye to his house for the last time and drove to Blanworth in the dark early morning, summing up his life as usual. He was fifty-three years old. He was an architect. He designed his house. He found the spot to build it in the leafy countryside between the towns of Blanworth and Toxon.

He had grown up in Blanworth with a contented childhood, decent parents - now deceased - and happy memories from school. He had met his future wife at college and, a few years later, they had had a daughter. But the marriage had disintegrated and, when his daughter had grown up, his wife had left him. But, a few months ago, his wife renewed some kind of friendship whilst finalising their divorce.

He was proud of Gowan Partnerships: set it up with his friend Pete Williams after working for an architectural firm for six years. Pete didn't have any cash, but John had money from his inheritance, so they used his name. As time went on they handled bigger clients; and eventually, they landed a deal with Zenith to design a large office block in the centre of Blanworth, replacing an old building destroyed by terrorists. Unfortunately, near the end of construction, Pete no longer wanted to work for Gowan Partnerships; and tomorrow, he would start a new company, taking most of their employees with him. Only John's long-standing PA, Janice, remained loyal to John, but his lack of interest in a future company meant she would be finding work elsewhere.

The city's lit buildings rose from the horizon as the countryside became flat. Near the illuminated arches and tall spires of the impressive cathedral, John's blurred building shimmered like a mirage.

Inside the shopping centre, few shops were open, but John found a café where he ate breakfast and watched early risers walking to work. About now, a delivery firm should be entering the Zenith building with two identical packages. John had been assured by Ronald, Head of Security and with whom John had been in contact the last few weeks, that the packages, already wrapped in party paper and ruined if opened, would be taken to the proper places. One would go to the first floor where people would continue celebrations after the initial festivities in City Square, and the other would be taken to the top floor where the select few, comprising mainly of Zenith staff and politicians, would hold their party at the end of the day.

John pushed through the doors leading onto City Square. The day was lighter now, and he avoided looking at The Freedom Building which lurked dominantly on the other side. Soon its pain would be over. A stage had been erected in front and had policeman and workmen around it. In a couple of hours, he would be sitting there with a few others giving speeches. Zenith wanted John to take part because, although they wanted people to believe that Pete solely designed the building which, indeed, many people did, neither John's nor Pete's contribution to the design had been proved, and omitting John would cause unnecessary controversy on a day that was supposed to celebrate the new building. The tramp was on the bench, staring at it.

'You were here the night I took measurements, a few days after the old building was destroyed,' John said.

'Aye, I remember.'

'And you were here when I fell and knocked my head, because you called the ambulance.'

'Hmm.'

'You were here either side of my amnesia, as if the world I entered for three and a half years was guarded by you standing at its entrance and exit.'

A cold breeze passed through the Square. There were still glimpses of stars in the morning sky. John shivered and closed his eyes for a moment, feeling almost at one with the expanse of the universe. The breeze whistled quietly in his ear like an angel enticing him to heaven. He didn't know what he was doing in this moment, nor why he was doing it, but he opened his eyes, turned to the tramp, got down on his knees and bowed. Tears flooded into his eyes and fell from his cheeks to the ground. The tramp grinned warmly at him, and John walked back to the café. As he did so, he received a text saying the packages had been delivered to the building.

Upon returning to the Square an hour later, with only a

couple of hours to go, a crowd had gathered. At the front of the crowd were yellow barriers and policemen, and in-between the barriers and the stage was a considerable gap where the press was setting up cameras and fiddling with microphones.

John knew he would not be able to see the overall appearance of the building if he tried looking now; but perhaps later today, when the symbol of freedom was burning to hell and the poison of its hypocrisy was dissolving inside him, he would. With this thought, adrenaline pumped through his body, and he lit a cigarette to calm himself before being let through the barrier by Security.

Wilkinson and Mann were at the stage. Mann stood confidently as ever, both legs straight and hands behind his back. Wilkinson appeared calm and detached, smiling amicably at John.

'You're joining us for the party afterwards, I gather.' Wilkinson said.

John wondered whether Ronald, Head of Security, had told Wilkinson about the packages: 'Yes, I'm looking forward to it.'

'Good, very good. I'm glad you can be with us today, despite our differences in the past.'

Pete approached and smiled cautiously at John: 'Haven't seen you for a while.'

'With no future for my company, there didn't seem to be much point in going to the office.'

Pete nodded with an embarrassed swiftness and adjusted

his glasses. Wilkinson and Mann looked away, pretending not to hear. The press had already reported that Gowan Partnerships was ending so Zenith didn't have to pretend they didn't know, but it seemed likely that Zenith approved of Pete's move; and perhaps, they even engineered it. Pete's decision to form another company and all the staff going with him had created further public suspicion that John had not designed the building.

'But I don't blame you for forming a new company, Pete,' John said, knowing that the building's destruction would amend all wrongs. 'It makes sense to distance yourself from me to gain better contracts.'

Pete raised his manicured eyebrows with surprise.

The four men ambled nervously for the next hour, drinking tea and watching the gathering of the crowd behind the barrier. People seemed joyful, but there were also political protesters, wearing t-shirts with topical messages, who were beginning to chant against the building. Over the past few weeks, their initial support for John, after the television and radio interviews, had waned because they, like those who supported Zenith, deemed his comments to be, at the very least, insensitive to the victims who died. Even Muslim extremists didn't support John because he had said he didn't support their cause.

Eventually, the four men were asked by organisers in yellow Hi Vis to sit on the stage where other dignitaries were beginning to sit. These included local and national politicians and the Blanworth Mayor with his ceremonial golden chains. A small selection of people who lost loved ones in the old building were also here.

At 11 a.m., in front of a protective screen of bulletproof plastic, the Prime Minister, with whom John had neglected to talk, rose from his seat and walked to a microphone in the middle of the stage. He was tall, broad and had the kind of thick hair that, no matter how well-cut, appeared scruffy.

'Ladies and Gentleman, it's with great happiness and delight that I am standing here today in front of the completed Zenith building.' There was applause. 'Five and a half years ago, this city and, indeed, this country were shocked by a horrible event but, in the aftermath, I was struck by the tenacity and bravery of the local people. Much praise has to go to the firemen, policeman, doctors and nurses who helped tirelessly after the attack, and also to you, the ordinary citizens who, in the days and weeks that followed, stood firm together, not letting it affect your daily lives. Your love, courage and endurance should serve as an example to us all.'

There was more applause as the Prime Minister turned towards the building behind him and raised his hand: 'What better monument could there be to the victims and their families than this wonderful, new building we have here.'

There were yet more claps, and he looked at his notes on the stand in front of him: 'It hasn't been without a little controversy, but I'm sure most people will agree that this building is a marvellous symbol of our country's values. I will now pass you over to the architects, Mr Pete Williams and

Mr John Gowan.'

He, evidently, hadn't intended to say much because Zenith's business practises, along with John's comments on television and radio, had become such a hot political issue that he needed to distance himself from them, as much as he could. He smiled and winked at Pete as he sat down. John followed Pete to the front of the stage.

'Thank you, so much,' Pete said, and the applause quietened. 'It is an honour to be here, with you today, and to be a part of something so important to this city.' It had been agreed by Pete, John and Zenith that neither man should say he designed the building: 'I feel terribly grateful, because without Zenith's belief in this building and, indeed, without the government's backing, which you, the taxpayer, paid for, this would never have been possible. Thank you, so much!'

There were claps, whistles and a few boos from the protesters at the back of the crowd. Pete sidestepped and John moved to the microphone.

John had prepared his short speech, and Wilkinson had approved it as part of today's agreement to be here. Zenith's PR lady had thought the speech a little odd, but she didn't object. If John, however, departed from it by even one word, there could be heavy legal repercussions because he had signed an agreement. Not wanting to jeopardize his operation today, in any way, and with the knowledge that his speech would be interpreted differently after today's events, he began reciting.

'Today is a momentous day and will be remembered for

many years to come. The building should, ideally, offer a guiding light for people to see, to feel, to experience. From the ashes of the last building and from the construction of this one, there will only be light! It hasn't been without controversy and, it's true, I helped fuel the fire. But, whether you embrace its light or not, I hope you can, at least, experience something from it today. Thank you.'

There was some applause, some silence and many boos. The public had, unsurprisingly, sided with Pete in the debate over who designed the building. How could they not? Their feelings were entrenched in the warm solidarity against terrorism. John's cause was altogether more elusive.

'Well done,' Wilkinson said quietly to John, clearly pleased he had kept to the approved script.

For the next thirty minutes, further speeches followed: first by Wilkinson, who said nothing that could be construed as political; then by relatives of the victims; and finally, by the Mayor, who praised local talent and local enterprise. At 11.40 a.m., on schedule, the men and women left the stage and stood to its side – at the centre of the Zenith building – with the press facing them in a huddled line.

At noon, the Prime Minister stood next to the red ribbon draped over the entrance, ready for the ceremonial cut. John guessed it was a shop entrance and not the main entrance, which would probably be down the side road – as with the previous building.

'To the future!' the PM shouted, with a grin aimed at the cameras, and he cut the ribbon to great applause.

John looked at his watch. There were only five minutes before his packages would ignite. He had gleaned the idea for an incendiary formula from a television documentary about Australian helicopter pilots who drop fire initiators onto woodland, to minimise the possibility of wild-fires. The initiators included a mixture of ethylene glycol and potassium permanganate that, when mixed together, cause an exothermic reaction.

The ethylene glycol was sold in a hardware store, and the potassium permanganate, on the Internet. On the particular website where he had bought it, a customer had warned purchasers of police attention, so John had been ready to justify the considerable quantity that he had bought for cleaning his pond – which was, indeed, especially foul and bug-ridden.

In each wrapped package a plastic tub contained a kilogram of potassium permanganate powder. On the underside of the lid was attached an upside-down, two-litre plastic bottle of liquid ethylene glycol. The bottle's tapering end was cut away and replaced with a thick layer of candle wax, which prevented the liquid from falling onto the potassium permanganate. Two light bulbs were attached to the candle wax. A battery timer, stuck to the box, was attached with wires to the bulbs. At the right time, the light bulbs would switch on, the wax would melt and, five minutes later, the ethylene glycol would gush through the melted wax, hitting the potassium permanganate powder.

Despite the exothermic reaction, John still needed to

do two things to give his fire the best chance of spreading – disable the sprinklers and stop the firemen from entering the building. He also needed to evacuate the building to make sure there were no fatalities. He guessed that the fire only needed a good ten minutes of blazing before the building was beyond help, but he wasn't an expert and had no way of knowing.

He stepped away from the other dignitaries, who were smiling at the cameras, and moved to the corner of the building, sufficiently away from people. By now, the light bulbs would be burning the candle wax. He phoned the police.

'Blanworth Police,' a bored female voice said.

'Now, listen very carefully,' he said, quietly but confidently. 'There are several bombs in the new Zenith building that will detonate today at different times. You have five minutes to evacuate the building.'

John said there were multiple bombs to reduce the possibility of the firemen going inside and tackling the blaze.

'I will send an email, immediately after this telephone call, with detailed information of the building, including password codes and photos of secret safe rooms, to confirm the validity of this threat.'

John had obtained this information from Janice over the past few weeks and, without looking at any of it, he had copied it all into one email.

'My email address is ******, and the email will be entitled "Bomb". If there is any attempt to enter the building, all the bombs will explode prematurely.'

'Who are you?' she asked, with a heightened pitch.

John ended the call and sent the email. He felt excited and turned to the crowd that was listening to another person speaking.

A minute later, a loud siren erupted through the building. The crowd stopped smiling and looked up with bemused faces. On his phone, John accessed a file, which he had obtained from Pete a few weeks ago, that controlled the building's sprinkler systems. With the press of a button, he turned them off.

Amidst the whirring noise of the alarm, he looked at his watch. The wax must have melted by now, and the ethylene glycol would have dropped into the potassium permanganate, causing an immediate exothermic reaction. The fire had begun!

A few people ran past him, coming from the side road – presumably, from inside the building. Soon, nobody would be inside. Everything was going to plan. People in the Square were holding their ears because the alarm was loud. They stared up at the building, not knowing what was happening. The police were trying to push them further back, away from the barriers, but they were slow to move. John was beginning to feel his heart race.

The dignitaries seemed bewildered and were being forced to move away quickly by police and bodyguards. Pete was shouting frantically to Mann over the noise, and Wilkinson appeared perplexed and quiet. The Prime Minister could not be seen.

'What's going on?' John asked, approaching Pete.

Pete turned from Mann and adjusted his colourful tie: 'A bomb threat, apparently. But nobody really knows yet. Where have you been?'

John smiled with a great sense of excitement and tapped him on the arm: 'The toilet.'

In the middle of the Square, the press were operating their cameras with expectant faces, like dogs waiting for their food.

'Mr Gowan, do you know what's happening?' a young black reporter shouted.

John avoided the press and approached the police barrier, where he stood for a few minutes. People were heaving forwards and sideways, and policemen were struggling to contain them. The alarm was loud enough to get people out of the building; but outside, people seemed to be drawn towards it. A voice, through a loudspeaker, was telling people to stand back, but it was hard to hear.

'Look!' somebody shouted. People were pointing towards something on one of the lower floors.

'Oh, a fire!' shouted another.

'Where?'

A huge whoosh of excitement spread through John's body, electrifying it. His first floor incendiary device had worked! An intense fire had spread through the room, lighting the party paraphernalia and extra sofas and chairs which he knew would be there for the party.

Fire engines were arriving in the Square, and the crowds

were forced to move aside. Their alarms were puny compared to the building's alarm, which seemed to pulsate in time with John's heart rate, uniting him with the fabric of everything. People appeared stricken, shocked. They were shouting, pointing and beginning to cry as they faced the prospect of terrorism, once more. John smiled and smiled.

Mann, Wilkinson and Pete joined John. From their steady stares, it was obvious they knew he was the culprit. John couldn't help but grin.

'Quite a spectacle,' Wilkinson said.

John nodded.

'Look there,' Mann said, pointing high in the sky.

A thin line of dark smoke slithered into the pale blue sky, curling and imitating the clouds. John's heartbeat increased as he realised it came from the top floor of the building, confirming that the other incendiary device had worked. He was, nevertheless, surprised at how quickly the building was burning.

'The fire is spreading quickly through the building,' Wilkinson said calmly, 'and smoke is funnelling through open windows at the top.'

'I do hope nobody's inside,' Pete said.

The alarm ended, and an eerie silence swept through the Square. Nobody was talking; some were crying; all were looking. The people, the Square and the black smoke that spiralled into the spring sun were united and whole, like the dark countryside and road in the moments before John crashed his car. There was a depth, a meaning, to everything that he saw: the way he experienced life as a child but with the addition of adult eyes that, far from sobering it, enhanced the truth of his experience. His heart had calmed down to a slow, undetectable throb.

'Aren't you going to look at it?' Pete asked John.

'I think I might.'

With the faith he would see the building and remember everything from the design process, he turned.